REBWAR

—————

DR GUL

OLS SCHABER

RORSCHACH PRESS

To my mother,
who made all this possible.

Dr Gul had just left his parked car on Vallance Road by a row of closed shops. He walked away and looked back to memorise the location: Shisha Store, Al-Safa Grill, a newsagent and a hairdresser. He carried on and took a left on Old Montague Street. The street lights lit the bare trees lining the road that led down to Brick Lane. Birds chirped away and he gazed up hoping to see some lucky stars in the clear night sky, but London's light pollution made it impossible. Dr Gul unzipped his jacket. He felt nervous and sighed to calm himself. He stopped and checked his watch: 2:14 am. He looked around to see a large tower block and rows of smaller two and four-storey buildings. Only a few of the flats had their lights on. Just by a parked car, a fox darted from a torn bin liner. Dr Gul carried on making sure the animal stayed away from him. He knew they carried a host of nasty diseases like roundworm, muscle worm, fleas and ticks.

He readjusted his shirt and jacket. The fox had found another bin bag to plunder along the road and Dr Gul carried on walking looking ahead. A taxi drove by and he looked down at the pavement. After a ten-minute walk, he arrived at Brick Lane. He hadn't spotted Mike Hays. Was he too early? He'd passed the drop-off point but there hadn't been anyone there. A white van turned into Old Montague Street. About halfway down, it took a left. Dr Gul walked towards it; a breeze had picked up and he zipped up. As he got closer he put on a black beanie cap and stopped. A fat balding man was putting on a high-vis jacket over his white overall and a hard hat. Dr Gul hid in the shadows just behind a parked car.

The man looked around him before opening the back of the van. Dr Gul spotted Hays' distinct braided goatee. He watched him set up a white pop-up work tent on the corner of the street with some street signs. It was the drop-off. Usually, he would wait for Hays to drive off, leaving the site unattended for precisely ten minutes. But today he was early. Once Hays had opened the manhole, Dr Gul walked over.

'Mike.'

Hays turned around and held his chest. 'Christ! You gave me a heart attack there. Mate, you're early.' He looked around. 'Come back—'

'I need four more boxes.'

'I can't. Look, come back for the pickup and we can talk another day. Can't be seen here.' A car accelerated down the street. Hays climbed down into the manhole. 'Quick... in. In!'

Dr Gul followed. The ladder led into an alcove that faced a sewer tunnel, which was lined with glistening uneven bricks. It was dark, damp and stank of London's waste. Dr Gul tried not to breathe and keep control of his gag reflex.

'Amin, we've been very clear about this. No, and no, understand? We can't pop up on the radar.'

'I need five boxes, otherwise, I am going to look elsewhere. My customers need more. Understand that, my friend?'

'Amin, calm... You're not drinking the Kool-Aid are you?'

Dr Gul looked at Hays' concerned face, but it only made him want to pull his ridiculous goatee and make him understand his position. 'Mike, I've talked to Steve and he said it was alright. Phone him.'

Hays shook his head. 'No, mate. I know what he said. Not pulling that stupid half-assed trick on me.'

Dr Gul grabbed Hays' white overall. 'I need them, now. OK?'

'Hello.'

They both looked up. Rain droplets dripped on their faces. Dr Gul could only see a faint backlit outline of someone looking down.

Dr Gul looked at Hays and pointed upwards.

'This not over.' Hays climbed up the ladder.

Dr Gul looked up and tried to listen in on the conversation, but it was being drowned out by the increasing flow of water in the sewer. He scaled up a few steps and a few more till he could hear that they were arguing. They were shouting at each other. Dr Gul looked up and saw Hays' fat screaming face falling towards him.

ONE

Geraldine had received a text message from her new Plan B contact, Highclere. It gave an address and a time. She'd made her excuses at work and gone out. Exited at Liverpool Street station and headed east towards Spitalfields Market. She remembered the old place where traders sold vintage clothes, antiques, knick-knacks and anything else that had value to a keen hoarder. It was chaotic, messy and original. She missed it. Now, though it still had a few of those eccentric stalls, it was more of a hipster affair. Regeneration they called it and they got some fancy architect to spruce it up. The locals had kicked up a fuss but lost to the mighty City of London. She crossed Commercial Street and passed The Ten Bells pub, where a Jack the Ripper tour was passing by. Tourists looked up, down and across, while listening to a bearded man wearing a light brown three-piece corduroy suit. The last time she had been on that tour was with her ex-husband when they were dating.

Her destination was Whitechapel Station, to which she could have gone directly, but she'd decided to make a walk of it. Geraldine liked to see the city on foot. It changed constantly and she enjoyed its transformations, even those that irked her. Fournier Street with its two-storey residential brick houses that led to Brick Lane had been kept intact. It still had some of those traditional curry houses. Back in the day, she would regularly visit one of them after a session at the pub, a Friday night tradition after a week on the beat. She was glad to see that they hadn't knocked down any buildings and had even left the colourful graffiti on the shutters. Hanbury Street turned into a typical post-modern residential development with its mix of grey flats and tower blocks.

Veiled mothers pushed their prams and shopping around. Since the fire at the Merkenstand mansion, Geraldine hadn't seen Rebwar. They had both thought that was the end of Plan B – it wasn't. On the drive back to London they were ambushed and taken in for questioning to some damp basement. They had been there for what had felt like days; Geraldine had soon lost all sense of time, never knowing even if it was day or night. They kept interrogating her, pushing for every detail, constantly. Eventually, she wasn't sure what she had said or what had really happened. She crossed Vallance Road and stopped. In front of her was a small park surrounded by three-storey apartment blocks and some shops – more veiled mothers with children. Traffic crawled around her. She took a few deep breaths. Her hands felt like clay as she held onto the handrail.

After a few deep breaths, she walked on down Vallance Road towards Whitechapel Road. Highclere had briefed Geraldine on what had happened to Plan B. He was her new contact. It was the official version or a variation of it. She guessed she'd never find out what had really happened. It had been an internal coup, Merkenstand had tried to take over the organisation and thus had ended up in a bloodbath.

Sir John Merkenstand had built an AI system that had infiltrated the organisation. The helicopter crash had been an assassination attempt that had nearly worked – Merkenstand had been turned into a vegetable – but, by then, the AI had taken over. When Rebwar and Geraldine had discovered the mansion, Plan B was on its knees.

Geraldine turned onto Whitechapel Road, a main artery into the City of London. Traffic rushed by her; the peace and quiet of the residential streets were now behind her. It wasn't long till she got to what looked like some roadworks. Some cones, a small easy-up, a couple of Thames Water vans and two men in high-vis jackets milled around a large manhole. Police vehicles were parked a bit further down – an unmarked black Vauxhall and a marked transit van.

'I'm looking for my colleagues.' Geraldine dug out her warrant card from her bomber jacket and flashed it.

One of the workmen smiled and looked down the manhole. 'In there.'

Geraldine stepped over the black hole.

'I'd get suited up if I were you,' said the other workman.

'Sorry?'

'It's a sewer.'

'Right...'

The man waved over to one of the larger vans and opened the back door. Hanging inside were sets of grey overalls, heavy-duty plastic boots, thick gloves and masks.

'Pick one, lady, and I'll help you down there.'

———

Geraldine was standing twelve feet under Whitechapel Road. She could still hear the murmur of the traffic above her. In front of her was a large dimly lit tunnel, big enough to drive a small van down. An ankle-deep brown river trickled slowly by her boots. The stinging odour hit and drilled into her nose and made her want to vomit. She tried to fight her senses, not knowing what her body wanted to do, wretch or run.

'You get used to it. Like anal sex...'

Geraldine turned to see the man laughing and showing a yellow set of teeth, which she was sure were rotten; she was glad she couldn't smell his breath. Why hadn't she noticed it above?

'This way, lady. Careful, it's slippery and you don't want to... you know. The last guy who swallowed a mouthful had to get his stomach pumped and he lost ten stone.'

Geraldine followed him, walking along as if she was on ice. She could see some torches ahead and hear some distant chatting, which echoed down the tunnel.

'I've got one of your colleagues here.'

Two men and a woman in full hazmat suits turned. Geraldine held out her gloved hand. They just waved back.

The woman talked through her mask. Geraldine stepped close to her. 'DC Pattel... and this is DS Gerrard and DC Fisher.'

Geraldine replied and glanced at what was behind them. It looked like a giant white rock. She hadn't noticed it before.

'It's a fatberg.'

Geraldine looked back at them.

'A fatberg.'

Geraldine looked at the rock and realised it was a giant ball of fat.

'Baby wipes cause them,' said DC Pattel.

'So... what's this all about?' Geraldine still fought the sickening smell.

'That.' DC Fisher pointed at a shape in the mass of fat.

Geraldine's eyes tried to work out what she was seeing. She stepped up closer. She could see some skin and some fabric. Her gloved hand touched the skin.

TWO

Rebwar walked out of the Day 1 Convenience Store on Wood Lane in Dagenham. He picked out a pack of cigarettes from a striped plastic bag he was holding, stood in front of a door and lit up. The street lights came on as he looked down the street towards the west. Behind the broken clouds, the sun was setting, giving off a warm red glow. Taking a drag of his cigarette, he walked off past some fenced off patches of green and heard the low thud of music. He looked at the time: 6:33 pm. He got out his keys and opened the door to a small, cream-coloured two-storey house. Its front garden was now a rough patch of cracked concrete with growing weeds, complemented by a rotting brown sofa set. He opened the door and a rumble of music beats and cannabis smoke escaped onto the street. Rebwar walked into the small hallway and past the living room door from behind which all the commotion was coming. He could hear voices in there too.

He walked into the kitchen. Every surface had something on it. Rebwar pushed some plates off the round central table and laid down his shopping. He sat on a chair and took out a can of beer from the bag. He opened it and took a large gulp then he undid his steel-toe-capped muddy boots and took off his black jacket. For a moment he let his thoughts wander and rubbed the back of his neck. It had been six months since Hourieh had left him and he hadn't seen her since. They had talked and Rebwar made sure he'd phone his son as regularly as he could. And he had let Hourieh have some space, as she had asked for. His instinct had been to find her and confront her, make her come back to her senses. But he knew her too well, she needed time to think things over. She had never been happy with the move to London from Tehran. But the situation there hadn't really improved. He lit another cigarette and his phone rang. It was Musa.

'Hey, son.'

'Hey, Dad. You still partying?'

Rebwar got up and shut the kitchen door. 'My noisy neighbour. I've just come back from my shift. It was an early one. Have you decided what you wanted for your sixteenth—'

'Dad!' Musa sighed. 'I... want you there. That's all.'

'Yeah, I know, I know. But you want a present? It's your sixteenth; big day. Are you going to bring your girlfriend?'

'Dad! No.'

'How's your mother?'

'Stressed.'

'How about you? School?'

'No, all good at school. Like my new maths teacher. No, it's... Oh, I don't know.'

'What? What's wrong.' Rebwar could hear Musa pacing around. 'Is she alright? Do I need to call someone to help?'

'It's... She's been trying to get in touch with Amin.'

'Dr Amin Gul?' Rebwar looked up and clenched his

jaw. He'd heard that she had been working for him. Dr Gul was an old acquaintance from Iran who had helped Rebwar in a missing person's case a couple of years ago when he had found a heart and needed it to be identified. Dr Gul then went through a messy divorce. 'Isn't she working for him?'

'Sort of… I mean… was.'

'What happened?'

The kitchen door opened and a black guy walked in wearing a yellow and green Brazilian football T-shirt and some jeans. His smile was broad and friendly. 'Hey, Mourinho, what's the score?' And he opened the fridge, which had a couple of Asda six-pack smart price lagers. He took one of them.

Rebwar covered the mic on his phone. 'Genny, can you—'

'Yeah, yeah old man. I'll calm the girls. Come in, my friend, and join us and you might enjoy yourself.' He stepped over to him. 'My friend likes you.' And he winked at him.

Rebwar pointed at his phone. 'My son.'

'Ask him over! Everyone is welcome.' Genny grabbed one of Rebwar's cigarettes. 'Light? Can I?'

Rebwar lit it for him and he left for his room.

'Son? You there?'

'Yeah. You know you can get me a video game.'

'What about Mum?'

'I only get to play after I've done my homework…'

Rebwar sat down again and the music got louder. 'Been watching football? Persepolis drew Esteghlal. Apart from five yellow cards, you didn't miss much.' This was considered the red-blue derby back in Tehran and, as soon as Musa could walk, Rebwar had taken Musa to watch Persepolis.

'I heard... Mum's calling.'

'Can I talk to her?' Rebwar heard Musa pace.

'I... I don't think... Dad, I don't...'

'I understand. But keep an eye on her. You're the man of the house, understand? And if she needs help it's important you give it – and tell me too. Did she...'

'Dad?'

Rebwar pinched the bridge of his nose and felt a moment of sadness pass over him. He drank some of his beer. 'Love you, OK?'

'Yeah, Dad. Love you too.'

'Take care, son.' Rebwar hung up and looked out of the window onto an overgrown garden with black bin bags and more discarded furniture. Above the neighbours' houses was the orange haze. The London night sky had awakened. He was glad he didn't have to go out and work. The kitchen door opened again and a man in a white hoodie and grey tracksuit trousers walked in.

'Hey, boss, how's it hanging?'

They fist punched each other.

'Hey, Jesus.'

Jesus was originally from Morocco but his parents lived in Spain. Thin and gaunt with dark eyes, he was in his late twenties. He had been a passenger in Rebwar's Uber a couple of months ago and he had rented a room out to Rebwar.

'Finished work? You should join the party. Genny has some friends over.'

'So I can hear. Been a long day.' Rebwar took out his wallet and gave Jesus two twenty pound notes, which he took and put into his pocket.

'Room still leaking?'

Rebwar shrugged and took out another cigarette, and

Jesus left the room, back to the party. Rebwar took out his phone and looked for Raj's number. It had been a while since he had talked to his nephew. Not since the manor fire, when Rebwar had been taken to a basement somewhere in London and interrogated over a couple of days – or so he thought. They had kept him there in darkness and used spotlights to interview him. Classic interrogation. They had wanted to know everything. There were about three or four different voices asking him questions. Some were men, others women; he couldn't see their faces. What had surprised him was the lack of physical violence. He had expected it. Then, on the last day, a man walked in again shining a bright light into his face and gave him a piece of paper. He had to sign it. It had been described to him as insurance.

The man told Rebwar to memorise the official version of the story, which was that Merkenstand had bought an AI system from China and had used it to take over Plan B's IT system. This led to a coup and an assassination attempt on Sir John Merkenstand, which his mother had plotted. Charlie had been recruited by her to take over the organisation. But the mother had a change of heart as her son had been left in a vegetative state and tried to use an AI computer to replace him. And it all went south. 'Uncle, long time no hear.' Some high-pitched giggles followed 'Wait, wait...' Rebwar heard Raj masticate. 'You want a favour?'

THREE

Geraldine was propped on the bar holding a pint of larger. Callaghan's pub on Chrisp Street looked sterile, like a green shoebox along a road of council houses. Everything was flaking off including its customers. Geraldine went in out of necessity. She needed a little stiffener before her next meeting. Her nerves were like taught piano strings. She was on her second pint. Two of the locals behind her had already tried to chit-chat with her. She eyed up the optics on the bar: spirits from yesteryear – they brought back memories of her going into pubs with her mum. Back then, smoke hid most of the imperfections and made for lighter moods she thought. Surely with Brexit, they'd bring back smoking. She took out her phone and scrolled till she found a number. Sighed and drank some more of her beer. The number had been given to her by Kingclere. It was Rebwar's. They hadn't seen each other since the manor fire. And that had been six, seven, maybe eight months ago. She didn't know what to think. She was dreading meeting him. No real reason, no bad blood, or disagreement or... or what? Like a long-distance relationship, it had somehow fizzled flat.

'You're not from here are you?' said a deep gurgly voice.

Geraldine turned around to face a white, balding man, his nose broken and cheeks puffed red. His white England T-shirt barely covered his belly.

'Is that a problem?' She drank some more of her beer.

'Just like to know new pretty faces. You married?' The man looked at her left hand.

Geraldine glanced around at the odd framed photos and the penny dropped. There was a series of black and white prints of the Krays. 'Is there a problem?' She spotted four tattooed dots on the man's hand.

'I know you, don't I?' The man squinted and studied her with his left eye. He was unsteady on his feet and was holding on to the bar.

'I don't think so. You are?' Geraldine tried to ignore him by looking around her.

'How's my old mate Marty...' The man snapped his fingers a couple of times. 'You know Marty, Marty Coats.'

Geraldine looked at the man. His small beady blue eyes were bloodshot and watery. It all came back like a kick to the head. DI Marty Coats her old boss. As old school as they came and when she got to know him she discovered he was burned-out like a forgotten cigarette. 'Michael O'Shea...'

'Geraldine Smith, I can smell a copper. I knew it.' O'Shea tapped his nose. 'Doesn't let me down. I'm still standing, aren't I?'

'And snitching?'

O'Shea stepped closer to her. 'Who's asking?'

DI Coats had had O'Shea on the Met's payroll but it was as more of a drinking buddy; his intel was barely credible. O'Shea would pass on gossip and headlines that he'd read in newspapers. Then when Coats needed results, would bring in the usual petty thieves and pin something on them. 'What did you go down for?'

'Stich up. Fucking stitched. That what it was. Where was he?'

Geraldine checked her watch and ordered another round.

'Are you sure?' said the barman, looking at O'Shea.

'Fuck off, Mick, I've got friends...'

To which the barman laughed and poured two Stellas.

'How's Marty?' said Geraldine.

'Went down to a sausage sandwich. Rest in peace.'

'Nah... I'll be damned! He did have an appetite. And you?'

'Sister.'

'What?'

'I lied for her and... long story.' Geraldine found herself holding back. How long ago was it? Fresh faced, single, ready to change the world. What had happened?

O'Shea stepped forward and waved her closer to him. 'Got any?' He licked his lips. '...You know. A few to get me over. Been a hard few months, if you know what I mean. I'll keep an ear out for you.'

Geraldine shook her head.

'Just a few loose ones... All right got a cigarette?'

Geraldine brought out a pack of cigarettes and parted with one. O'Shea's hand trembled as he placed it between his ear and his greasy white hair.

'Armed robbery, wasn't it?'

O'Shea tilted his head as he was hard of hearing.

'Fifteen and good behaviour. Right?'

'Stich up! I wasn't even there.'

'Did they ever find out who was behind those fine art thefts?'

O'Shea turned over to the bar and looked towards the door. She'd have to pay for that, although it would only be part of another story. Geraldine had a sneaking suspicion that DI Coats had been involved in that racket too, but she wasn't here to dig up the past. She drained the last of her pint and left the pub.

FOUR

Rebwar had been blindfolded. All he was aware of was a musty smell that could have been coming from him. He hadn't shaved or showered since he had been to that village outside the Merkenstand Manor. He was tired, sore and disoriented. He could only remember getting into the outskirts of London and a van overtaking and blocking them. Four cagoule-clad men stepped out all dressed in black combat gear. Each one pointed a Heckler & Koch G36 which, the Met police used. Rebwar and Geraldine were hooded and cable tied. After a long and bumpy ride, they stopped somewhere and were led into a building with multiple doors and stairs. It smelled damp and woody.

They both had reckoned that something like this would happen. They had managed to sneak out of the data centre that Charlie, Geraldine's Plan B handler, had broken into to steal millions of users' data. Charlie had masterminded a trap that made Geraldine and Rebwar look like they had gone rogue and decided to rebel against Plan B. With a hired gang called the Filthy Five, Charlie had made them chase a merry-go-round of crimes. None of them made sense but she had made sure Rebwar and Geraldine were at the right place at the wrong time. It all looked to Plan B that they had committed the crimes. And now that had caught up with them.

Rebwar felt the heat of two bright lights shine towards him. Then came the sound of boots and metal chairs dragged along the floor.

'Rebwar Ghorbani.'

Rebwar turned towards the voice.

'Nod if correct.'

He did.

'We are Plan B.'

'Who's we?'

'You were at the Merkenstand Manor with DS Smith.'

'Yes.'

'And what was the purpose of your visit?'

'Charlie told us to go there.'

'Mrs Charlie Atkins aka the Ferret.'

'Yes.'

Rebwar heard a few whispers around him and guessed that there were about three people in the room. His hands were tied to the back feet of the metal chair.

'What was the purpose of the visit?'

'To break in.'

'Why?' said a voice to his left. It was deeper and had an accent that he didn't recognise. 'What was the mission or assignment?'

'Charlie didn't tell us. We had to take Daisy Merkenstand with us. She was part of the Filthy Five.'

One of the men got up and walked towards a door, which opened with a creaking metallic sound.

'Why did you go along with the mission?'

'We decided the only way to stop her without giving Plan B away was to go along with her instructions.'

'So you committed murder, extortion and robbery to stop her?'

'That was her plan, she used the Filthy Five to carry out her crimes. And made it look like it was us.'

'Double bluff,' said the second man.

'Who is Charlie?'

'Plan B contact. Ask DS Smith – it's her contact.'

The door opened and someone walked in and went up to the men and whispered something.

'When did you know that you were being set up?'

'By Charlie?'

'Yes.'

'I suspected when she asked me to set up Geraldine but didn't realise that she was committing crimes around us.'

'Mr Ghorbani why should we believe you? We have four dead agents and a trail of destruction. As to who looks the guilty party... well how best to say it. Guilty as charged.'

'Can I call my family or at least someone...' Rebwar felt a sense of despair. They were just going to sweep this whole sordid affair under the carpet with him under it. 'Can I get a drink?'

'Let's go back to the data centre. Who was there?'

'Pinky Knight, Joseph Brunje and Charlie – what was left of the Filthy Five.' Rebwar heard the ruling of paper over at a desk.

'And Daisy Merkenstand?'

Rebwar licked his dry lips. 'What about that drink?' He heard some whispering and the movement of chairs and desks. A man walked up and removed his hood. Rebwar's eyes stung as the intense spotlights burned into the back of his *eyes. He looked down feeling the sharp pain dissipate. Slowly, as if watching a tyre inflate he regained his sight. Squinting in front of him he could only see two bright lights with a void of black behind them. Beside him was a table with a glass with water and a straw. He leaned in and slowly sucked the clear liquid that tasted like a sweet, refreshing elixir. It momentarily washed away his pain and tired muscles.*

'I'll ask again,' the voice came from behind the lights. 'Daisy?'

'Last we saw of her was riding a horse. She had been used as a pawn by Charlie. Think she suffered from Stockholm syndrome. You had her in custody with Charlie... Remember after we found her with O'Neil?' Plan B had asked him to find the gipsy in a previous operation that led to a people trafficking gang run by Richard O'Neil who had been involved with Plan B. Rebwar smiled at them. 'See a pattern?'

'And you discussed all this with DC Smith?'

'Yes.'

'Even though it was expressly forbidden to interact with your handlers.'

'Got a cigarette?'

A man emerged from the darkness wearing a balaclava and offered Rebwar a cigarette. The man lit it for him and Rebwar puffed and felt the pleasure of a long-lost friend. It soothed and eased the moment. With his lips, he shuffled it carefully to one side of his mouth. He was going to try and savour it for as long as he could.

'Mr Ghorbani,' said another voice, 'we're going to take a tea break and then we'll carry on with our chat.' Chairs scraped on the concrete floor and footsteps made their way to a door. Rebwar carried on savouring the last millimetres of his cigarette. So far he'd been surprised, it was as if they were trying to join the pieces of a puzzle. Charlie had really pulled

the wool over their eyes. He wondered how this would play out. There were a few scenarios. Some weren't worth thinking about, others required a degree of falsehoods and trust in him. Charlie had done a good job discrediting both of them. The door's hinges shrieked open. This time it was a mix of boots, shoes and high heels. He had no idea how much time had passed.

'Mr Ghorbani,' said a deep slow voice. 'We have some paperwork for you to sign. Then I am going to leave you with... some of my colleagues to work out your story. Do you understand what I have just asked you to do?'

Rebwar nodded.

'Can you for the record say yes and state your name.'

Which he did and the man left the room. Silence remained except for a couple of coughs. The man wearing the balaclava arranged the table with the water to face him and undid the handcuffs. He laid out two sets of stapled paper and a pen and returned behind the lights.

A woman's voice called him. 'Mr Ghorbani, you will find a statement with its copy in front of you. I am asking you to read one and sign both. Do you understand what I have just said? Please confirm with a yes or no and your name please.'

Rebwar did so and squinted, trying to read the text. 'Sorry, can someone read this out?'

The woman began to read it.

FIVE

Rebwar was in his little booth by the main gate to a large construction site on Chrisp Street in Poplar. A big residential block was being built that offered luxurious apartments with views over the city. A bellowing horn got Rebwar's attention. A truck with a skip was waiting for the gate to be opened. Rebwar grabbed a clipboard, put on his coat and high-vis jacket and went over to the cab.

'Doing a double shift?' said the driver. 'Saw you this morning.'

Rebwar yawned. 'Bills don't pay themselves.' He passed the clipboard, which the man signed and passed it back. 'How's the little one?'

'Better. Got some pills. It's only worry, worry. Look.' He pointed to his greying hair and the truck pulled away.

Rebwar signed the paperwork and opened the large metal gate. He walked out into the road to help the truck pull out onto the street. As it drove off, he spotted Geraldine. He stepped back onto the pavement and closed the gate. 'What are you doing here?'

'Hey, Rebs.'

'You got sent?'

Geraldine shrugged and Rebwar squeezed the edge of the cold metal gate. She looked down at her Doc Marten shoes. 'They... Got some time?'

Rebwar looked at his watch and nodded. He went back into his little cabin and called for his boss, explained that he had to go and that his shift had ended a couple of hours ago. After a moment of silence, the man shouted back that he should wait till someone came to relieve him. Rebwar just responded that it wasn't his problem.

'Pub?'

'Let's walk first. OK?'

'OK. You OK?'

Rebwar shrugged and lit up.

'Dr Amin Gul,' Geraldine said. 'You know him?'

Rebwar nodded. He wanted to hear this.

'They've found his body.'

Rebwar stood there looking at her. Was this to get his attention? How could she know that he had asked Raj to look for him?

'In a fatberg.'

Rebwar waited for her to expand.

'It's disgusting... A huge ball of fat that clogs up the sewers. As big as one of those and sometimes bigger.' Geraldine pointed at a passing double-decker bus.

'But he wasn't my friend. I hated him... Oh you think...'

'Highclere sent me here. Plan B.'

'Pub?' Plan B were back and wanted him. He wondered what they were going to offer him this time. They hadn't deported him, must have reckoned he'd grown indifferent to his immigration status and he had grown used to it.

Geraldine looked up and down the street and consulted her phone. 'Still got your taxi?'

Rebwar shook his head.

———

After a few minutes walking, they were sitting around a small wooden table at the Festival Inn just around the corner from Callaghan's. Rebwar faced Geraldine with crossed arms and waited for her to start.

'I'm sorry...'

'For?'

'Oh, all this shit. How's Hourieh and Musa?'

He sighed. 'Left me and I haven't seen my son since then either. Maybe they could help find her.'

'I'm sorry to hear. Are you OK?'

Rebwar looked around and wanted to shout, scream, cry, laugh, smash someone. 'It's been lonely, though of... What about Dr Gul?'

'He's on a slab being tested. They want you to look into it. Did you know him?'

'Yeah, and my wife too. She worked for him. Arrogant man. He wasn't nice. I think that is why she wanted to work for him. Wind me up... Hey, maybe she did it. Am I a suspect?'

'He was found by Thames Water engineers who were removing the fatberg. Reckon he'd been there for a couple of weeks. Found some boxes of opioids. He could have committed suicide. What kind of doctor was he?'

'Plastic surgery. Has a practice... Two or more weeks? Wasn't he missed?' Rebwar leaned back against the wall behind him. 'No, no, I'm not getting sucked into this... it's no.'

'But you don't have an option.'

'What are they going to do? Deport me? Lock me up? Sue me? I mean... So what? I don't care anymore.'

'What about your son? Sure you could get shared custody...'

Rebwar laughed, coughed, drank some of his beer and let it settle him. 'You think the British are going to look after me? Why? They have been meddling with Iran for over a century. No, no, they have been playing since the beginning. I'm sure they somehow convinced me to come over here...' Geraldine was looking into her pint waiting for Rebwar to finish. 'I can't say I've been welcomed here can I? And now they've taken my family away.'

Geraldine nodded and sipped her beer. 'Do you want to go back?'

Rebwar looked out of the window and thought about it. He had considered it and reached out to some of his friends back home. But with all the sanctions, you had to be rich and privileged to have a decent life there. They did say he should go to Turkey or America. But what kept him here was Musa. He couldn't just leave him here.

'Dr Amin Gul.'

Geraldine smiled at him.

SIX

Geraldine was awaiting her fate in an unknown cell that she had been put in after being taken from a van with Rebwar. They had been separated as soon as they arrived at an undisclosed destination. She had been hooded and brought to a cell-like room, where she was sat on a wooden chair with her hands handcuffed to it. The smell of damp was overpowering and it felt cold, which made her shiver. She had been in two minds about shouting out her discomfort. All she knew was that a bunch of men in balaclavas had apprehended them, suspecting them of being Plan B operatives. Geraldine felt exhausted, physically and mentally. Her eyes kept wanting to shut but her thoughts kept racing, asking her endless questions. She was sure that the whole Charlie mess wasn't over and that there was more to come.

A key turned in a door in front of her. Boots paced towards her and behind. Furniture and chairs were moved around her.

'Hello?' she said to no response. 'Can I get a warm drink?'

They left the room and locked the door.

Geraldine sighed. She knew a little about Plan B's theatrical games. If it was them. She'd been to a few interviews with them and so had Rebwar. But this one felt a little more acute. She felt herself trying to drift off and felt her head drop. She tried to get up but felt her hands tugged to the chair and sat down again. The door squealed open and someone came in.

'DC Smith.' The man's voice was deep and rough.

'Yes.'

She heard a chair scrape as he sat down. 'I'm here to interview you.'

'Can I get a hot drink?'

The man sighed, got up and went up to the door. 'Tea and sugar?'

'Anything...'

He sat back down. 'Before we start, are you OK?'

'Not really. Can you remove the hood?'

'Not yet, sorry. What happened?'

'What do you mean?'

'Charlie?'

Geraldine heard some paper being moved around in front of her. 'She framed us.'

'How?'

'By asking us to do suspect jobs and making us walk into situations that made us look like the guilty party.'

'You could have said no.'

Geraldine laughed. 'No? To Charlie or Plan B?'

'Or contacted the police.'

'And you think they would have done something other than arrest us? We looked guilty as sin.'

'But you could have.'

'Look, Mr...?'

The man shuffled some papers in front of him. 'So what happened?'

'Charlie, your operative, pulled the wool over your eyes and tried to rob the Merkenstand company of their data.'

The man clicked a ball pen and she heard the sound of it being used. 'When did you become aware of this?'

The door opened and there was a shuffling of shoes and the rattling of a cup and saucer. This surprised Geraldine; who still served tea in that fashion? She could smell the distinct hay-like scent of sweet tea.

'DC Smith... the question...'

'Of the robbery, very late on. She nearly fooled us and we had to act quickly before they could get away.' Geraldine could nearly taste the drink. 'Mind if I get my tea?'

'Just a few more questions... your sister?'

'What about her?'

'The file says that you compromised your career for her.'

'Family. And I'm still paying for it, as you well know.' Geraldine had planted some evidence for her sister, Rachel, so she could get her revenge on her friend, Jordan who was sleeping with her boyfriend Zane. She should have known better than to try and help lowlifes like them but blood was thicker than water.

The man stood up and took Geraldine's hood off. She squinted at the strip lights above her. In front of her was a tall black man, well built, in a black polo neck. He had a prosthetic left hand and wore sunglasses, which partially covered his scarred eyes. For a moment she wondered if he was blind. He got up, walked behind her, and freed her right hand from the handcuffs.

'You can drink your tea.'

Her hand shaking, Geraldine picked up the dull white cup, which was lined with a heavy burgundy stripe – a classic canteen style which she had seen in numerous police stations and government offices. It gave a weird feeling of reassurance, something familiar that felt homely. The tea was strong and bitter with only the sweetness cutting in for a respite. It had probably been poured from one of those urns that stewed for days.

'We have prepared an official statement for you to sign.' The man used his prosthetic hand to push the paper to her.

Geraldine leaned forward, pulling on her handcuff to get as close as she could. On the paper was written: By signing below, I hereby acknowledge that I have read, understand and agree to the terms of this document relating to case No 09-437-897PB. I also affirm the truth of the following statement. She carried on reading and realised that it said that she had colluded with Charlie to compromise Plan B and steal from them. 'Sign these lies?'

'It's insurance. If you want to carry on working for us we need you to sign this. And move on. Understand?'

Geraldine knew this was non-negotiable. They had made that clear when they first recruited her. This is how they controlled their operatives and how she squared with it was that at least she was still a police officer. 'What assurance have I got that this isn't going to happen again?'

'We've made changes.'

The man leaned back and Geraldine spotted his black and white striped socks. 'You'll need to release me for me to sign it.'

He opened a file and flicked through the pages till he found what he wanted. He took a key from his trouser pocket and released her left hand from the handcuffs. Geraldine picked up the pen and signed the document. The man then put the documents away in their folder.

'I'm your new contact.' He sat down and crossed his legs,

picked some fluff off his trousers. 'You can call me Highclere. Same rules apply for you. Nothing has changed. Understand?'

Geraldine nodded.

'You will take a few days of sick leave.' Highclere pushed over another file to her. 'In there is your cover story. Medical depression. In there is a doctor's note and here is your medication.' He reached into a case by his chair and pulled out a box of pills. 'Placebos.'

Geraldine picked up the box and laughed. 'Prozac? I might need the real stuff... Joke.'

Highclere pushed his sunglasses back onto the bridge of his nose. 'Good luck. You'll be reporting to me in the next few days.' Highclere cleared out his desk and banged on the door. It was quickly unlocked and he left. Geraldine sipped the now lukewarm tea.

SEVEN

Geraldine was walking with a bag of shopping along Gayville road. A gust blew a confetti-like load of leaves around her. A few of the wet leaves stuck to her and she peeled one of them off her black bomber jacket. Like death, she found autumn depressing even its bright colours made her melancholic and lethargic. She missed the sun's warm energy and power. She stopped and realised that she had passed the flat. She fumbled for her key but, before she could find it, a man opened the door. He wore Lycra and a cycle helmet and his shoes made him walk like a penguin, which always made her laugh.

'Hi.'

'Hi,' Geraldine replied. She'd forgotten his name and, from his hurried getaway, he had forgotten hers too. She did remember he was a student from China – or studying Chinese, again, something that she'd forgotten. She opened the door to the ground floor flat and walked in. She put her shopping on the table in the kitchen which overlooked a long green garden. She got an IPA beer can out of the plastic bag and opened it; took a big slug and looked out onto the houses that backed the garden. Some soft steps came closer to her and she felt a kiss on her neck. It sent a shiver down her spine and she gave in to the embrace. Hands touched and rubbed her breasts and belly. Teeth nibbled her ear. A hand rubbed her hard nipple.

'I...'

She kissed her. The semi-darkness faded away into pleasure, her body feeling alive with animal energy. She felt her jeans being undone and she was being pushed towards the wall. Blonde hair trailed down over Geraldine's breasts and over her belly and she felt a kiss and tongue over her tingling flesh. She was hers. She had lost control to her. All her senses wanting her. The kissing travelled lower past her belly. She wanted her. All of her. Geraldine's phone buzzed and reverberated; it was in her jeans pocket. But her jeans were now over her ankles and on the black slate floor. Geraldine held the blonde hair pushing and pulling. Wanting the passion but wanting to take the call. The pleasure and guilt played in her mind. The phone stopped ringing and Geraldine held onto a kitchen counter, her body giving in to the pleasure as she gasped for air. The phone buzzed again and the guilt returned – and now worry. It had to be important. She tried to block it but couldn't.

Geraldine broke away and picked up the phone. 'Hi.' She pulled up her jeans. 'How are you?'

'Good, good. And you.'

Geraldine looked back, a beautiful blonde woman stared back at her. She was smiling and about to laugh. Geraldine signalled to her with her index finger to be quiet. The woman brushed back her long blonde hair. She was slim and had big blue eyes. For a forty-something her soft wrinkles were sexy. Her dressing gown was loose and flashed skin.

'Yeah, good—'

'Is someone there?'

'No, no. Look, Becks, have you read that report?'

'Babes, you know I miss you... Can I see you?'

Geraldine looked up at the ceiling. 'I... I'm busy but how about a drink?'

The woman got up and adjusted her bathrobe making sure it was tight around her slim body. She opened the fridge and took out a pack of orange juice.

'OK, about the report. It's interesting... And a practising doctor. He was a smoker, drank, took lots of supplements, didn't take opioids. He's been hit over the head, which probably caused the fall, and then he drowned in the sewer.'

'When did he die?' Geraldine took a sip from her beer can. The woman put the kettle on. Geraldine nodded yes to a tea.

'Oh... About four weeks ago... that fat slowed the decomposition. You know they find more body-building steroids in the fatberg than cocaine. I blame Instagram... And he's got some scratches on his back. Which were made... by a woman.'

'How?'

'Sex, she...'

Geraldine looked at the blonde woman's red nails. She had felt those. 'OK, how do you think he got in there?'

'You're going to have to invite me for dinner for that.'

'You're such a tease. Can I bring a friend?'

'G... I want you. Who is it?'

'Sandra...'

Sandra turned around and smiled at Geraldine, her

perfect white teeth showing as she stuck out a pierced tongue. It made Geraldine shiver with excitement.

'And?'

'It'll be a surprise for all three. I'll text you. OK? Kisses.' Geraldine hung up.

Sandra went over to her and kissed her. 'You're such a tease... Is that the Beckie?'

'Yeah.' Geraldine smiled.

'You can't play us off against each other.'

Geraldine thought about it for a moment. She wanted both of them. 'Why not?'

'Listen, I might be a piece on the side and I get that you've been through the mill. But no.'

'No?'

'No.'

Geraldine looked around for a cigarette.

'And you're going to have to give those up if you want to be with me.'

EIGHT

Rebwar stood in front of an office block. A series of shiny brass plaques stared back at him. He buzzed a company called KhanWin Beauty. A woman's voice replied over the intercom and asked who it was. Rebwar said that he had a meeting with Dr Edwin Norwin. The door clicked and he pushed it open. At the reception was a brunette wearing glasses and with painted eyebrows and pouty lips.

'Mr...?'

'Rebwar. I'm a friend of Dr Gul.'

'Oh, he's not working for us anymore. You sure it wasn't Dr Khan you wanted to see? He's free.'

Rebwar had known that, as Dr Felber had mentioned, Dr Gul had left under a cloud and had been a partner at KhanWin Beauty.

'What procedure is it regarding?'

Rebwar watched her frozen smile. It was as if she wasn't in control of her facial expressions. Rebwar read her name badge. 'Attesa, I'd rather talk with Dr Norwin.'

'Yes...' She picked up the phone still wearing the frozen

smile. 'Rebwar, a friend of Dr Gul... Yes...' She looked up at Rebwar. 'What is it about?'

'He's gone missing.'

She repeated the message at which Dr Norwin agreed to see Rebwar.

Dr Norwin's office was a shiny white apart from a few plants and some reference books to break the intensity of the clinical feel. The doctor's tanned face looked huge and contrasted with the white lab coat that was tight around his slight frame.

'Mr Rebwar. Please sit. What can I do for you? Coffee?'

'Espresso, please.' Rebwar shook Dr Norwin's hand. He had a light grip and his palm was dry.

Dr Norwin called reception for the coffee. 'You would like to have some cosmetic changes? Injury or accident?'

'It's about Dr Gul. Do you know where he is?'

Dr Norwin sat back in his tall white designer chair and interlocked his fingers. 'Dr Gul?'

Rebwar nodded.

'Well... He worked here, yes. But we parted ways.'

'When was that?'

'Sorry, but what's that got to do with anything?'

'He's a friend.'

'Well... I... I don't know. We parted ways.'

The door opened and a woman in a white lab coat with short red hair walked in with his espresso.

'Llaria, thank you. This is Llaria Boyd. Mr Rebwar is asking about Dr Gul.'

Ms Boyd placed the cup on a glass table next to Rebwar. 'Dr Amin Gul, handsome man. Proud and liked the women.'

Dr Norwin stopped in mid laugh. 'Did he? You know?'

'Edwin, I told you. Yes, he tried it on but I said no and he stopped. Said I had a fiancé.'

Rebwar searched her hands but they were bare of any jewellery. 'You know my wife worked here too.'

Both turned their heads to Rebwar.

'Hourieh Ghorbani.'

'Hourieh! Ahh...' Dr Norwin smiled.

Ms Boyd gave a nervous smile, her bright green eyes staring at Rebwar. 'Yes, she was assisting Dr Gul.'

'Yes, yes I remember now. She was...'

Rebwar looked over at Dr Norwin. 'When was that?'

He tilted his head and looked at Rebwar. 'She's your wife?'

'She's left me.'

'Mr Rebwar, sorry, but we don't offer therapy sessions here.'

'I need to find them.'

Ms Boyd hid a smile with her hand.

'She could be in danger,' said Rebwar. She has my son, Musa.'

Dr Norwin pushed back on the shiny white desk and his chair rolled back. 'Mr Ghorbani, I would strongly advise you to report this to the police and find a solicitor.'

'Ms Boyd, was my wife having an affair with Dr Gul?'

'Uh...' She tried to hide a nod with a shake of her head. 'They argued and he fired her. It was an awful scene. Awful.'

'Llaria, I think Mr Ghorbani needs to leave. I have a busy day here.'

'Opioids.'

'Sorry?'

'I've heard rumours and—'

'And what?' Dr Norwin stood up. 'I am not going to let

anyone come here and accuse me of any nonsense... malpractice... or... or... Do you understand?'

'Why do you say malpractice? Is that the reason why Dr Gul left?'

'Ms Boyd get Dr Khan here to escort Mr Ghorbani off the premises. I'm not having some jealous man bring his dirty washing here.'

'There's something you are hiding. I know and will find out.'

Dr Khan walked in. He was a big balding Indian man. His round face looked like it was going to explode. 'What's going on here?'

'Mr Ghorbani is about to leave and—'

'I'm looking for my wife and Dr Gul.'

Dr Norwin grabbed Rebwar's arm. His grip was surprisingly weak and he could barely hold on.

'I demand to know what happened to my wife. Why was she sacked? You know I will get myself a solicitor and sue for unfair dismissal. Did she find out something about Dr Gul? Is that why there was a fight?'

'Vivek, don't say anything,' said Dr Norwin. 'He's just a sad jealous man looking to do us harm.'

'Hourieh is your wife?' said Dr Khan. 'She did mention you... you're ex-police and a private detective.'

'Get him out!' Dr Norwin tried to pull Rebwar out of his office.

'Edwin, wait we... wait,' said Dr Khan.

Dr Norwin stomped over to his desk and picked up the phone and dialled. Dr Khan pressed on the catch to end the call. 'Let's think.'

The two stared at each other. Rebwar watched Dr Khan trying to calm the situation.

He turned to face Rebwar. 'Let's start again. I'm Dr

Vivek Khan and this is my partner and Ms Boyd is our clinic manager. And I think if you would like any assistance from us then you should contact our solicitor. Because of client confidentiality, we cannot give you any more information.'

'I am going to find out. You understand? Don't you care that Dr Gul is missing? He might be dead!'

Dr Khan laughed and the others joined in nervously. 'Mr Ghorbani, I think your matrimonial jealousy may have left you with issues. Dead? Come on, if anyone would be guilty of such thoughts and accusations it would be yourself, don't you think? Now leave or we will call the police.'

Rebwar made his way out of the office and smiled at the receptionist, who was still smiling and typing on her computer.

NINE

Geraldine had come early to Café Rouge in Dulwich. It had been where she had met Beckie for their first date and she had insisted on it. It felt like that had been in another life. What was she thinking? You couldn't mend past mistakes or live in the past. Geraldine had moved on or so she thought. Sandra was her new woman. She could certainly scratch an itch. But did she deliver what Beckie did? But then what was that? Geraldine looked around her. The restaurant was slowly filling with couples and friends. Giggles, smiles, a high five and laughter. The place was starting to buzz. A blackboard displayed the specials and the times of happy hour. It had just started.

'Drink?' said a tall thin man with crooked teeth.

Geraldine looked around and saw people drinking beers and cocktails. 'Two margaritas.'

The waiter nodded and turned away. Geraldine checked her reflection in the mirror next to the table. She hadn't made much of an effort and searched her pockets for a lipstick. She looked tired and got up and went to the toilet to find two girls chatting to each other as well as adjusting their make-up. Geraldine went over to one of the basins and splashed her face with cold water. The two girls stared.

'Nice lippy,' said Geraldine.

'Thanks, it's Dior. Want to try it? Got a spare.' The dark-haired girl was wearing a little too much make-up.

'Sure.' Geraldine wiped her face with a paper towel and took the lipstick. She hadn't intended on trying to borrow someone else's make-up and it was not something that most girls would offer up – but needs must.

'Try some of this.' The dark-haired girl got some sample products out of her large handbag. 'I'm in the cosmetic department at Debenhams.'

Both girls tilted their heads and smiled at Geraldine. The slim brunette girl with painted eyebrows stepped up. 'Can I?'

Geraldine nodded and with excited giggles, they applied make-up on her. She wasn't sure if they felt sorry for her or it was just a reflex since they did this every day.

'Who's the date?' said the dark-haired girl.

'It's a meeting... my ex.'

'Complicated?'

Geraldine nodded.

'Oh, then, he'll be regretting dumping you,' said the tall brunette.

'She. And I dumped her.'

They giggled. 'More to you, girl,' said the dark-haired girl.

Geraldine had been transformed and had mixed feelings about what she was seeing. She hadn't been expecting this or planned it. She wanted to wash it all off and go home and curl up in front of the TV.

'Too much?'

'No, no, just not used to this attention. Looks amazing.'

'Ahh, thanks.' And the tall brunette kissed her cheek. 'Good luck, girl. No regrets, hey?'

Geraldine nodded and walked back to her table. Beckie was there sipping one of the two cocktails. Geraldine sat down and they stared at each other.

'Hi.' Beckie got up and kissed Geraldine's lips. 'You look gorgeous... I'm speechless.'

Geraldine looked at her reflection and had a hard time recognising herself. She looked younger, fresh faced, and sexy. 'Hi, Becks.' She raised her cocktail and cheered. Beckie still had that natural sexy beauty. Olive skin, big dark eyes. The memories flooded back good and bad. Her heart skipped a beat as if a child trying to learn a drum. Beckie grabbed Geraldine's hands. Nervously, she looked around and saw the two girls who were watching her and smiling.

'You know I still love you?' said Beckie. 'And I'm clean. Been for a while now. I'm good.'

Geraldine tried to break away from her grip. 'It's complicated.'

'Life is. And you must feel something for me. I mean, is that a mask you're wearing?'

'Babes... What about the report?'

'Always work, work.' Beckie sipped her cocktail. 'Sorry, I know... Guilty as charged.' She took another taste of her drink. 'Well, Dr Gul's scratches were made by a woman and from the scabs, they happened before. Even a couple of weeks before, I would say.'

'It's sexual?'

Beckie nodded and smiled. 'And I looked into those boxes of opioids that were found with him. They're from a company called Poroxy Inc. Heard of them?'

Geraldine shook her head.

'One of the major players for pain relief and a ticking time bomb for the NHS. Basically, legal heroin and it gets prescribed after surgery. And as addictive. Massive problem in America and becoming one here.'

'Were you on it?'

Beckie looked over her glasses. 'Something similar. Now they think there were about five or more boxes with hundreds of pills. That's a lot even for a doctor to have.'

'But you can have stock as a doctor?'

'A pharmacy would have, but again not on that level. And if you need more then it gets delivered. He must have been smuggling them.'

'So he was hit over the head and then fell into the sewer and then he drowns... Why leave all the opioids? Not a robbery is it? Or did it go wrong?'

The waiter came and asked them if they wanted to eat. Geraldine asked for another round of drinks.

'My first impression was that he slipped and knocked himself out. But from the blow you need to find the wall to confirm that.'

'Signs of a struggle?'

Beckie shook her head. 'Some bruising on his arms and legs. But not consistent with a fight.'

'So not a police baton. Why didn't anyone miss him? You'd think someone would have called the alarm. Anything else in there? Fingerprints?'

'No, the sewer cleaned all that away... Been seeing anyone?'

Geraldine looked around her and leaned back. 'It didn't work out... And...'

'G... I'm better now.'

Geraldine looked at her reflection and sighed. 'Shit, shit... I just don't know. I don't want to get hurt or hurt you.'

'Isn't that too late? Let's try again. I love you...'

Geraldine closed her eyes and let that sink in, hoping things would just fade away. She took a moment to search her feelings and leaned in to kiss Becks, who responded by grabbing the back of her head.

TEN

Rebwar sat in a cafe not far from KhanWin Beauty, watching the waiter wiping and aligning the tables. It was 6:55 pm and about to shut. Rebwar said his goodbyes and took the Metro newspaper he had been reading. Marylebone was an affluent neighbourhood with the famous Harley Street running down the middle of it, which had every top medical specialist there. You could understand why they had a practice there. Their clientele were in the streets, dressed immaculately in well-fitted clothes. Dr Gul had always worn tailored suits and he liked to make sure that everyone knew. A clever way of saying, I can make you look beautiful too. Rebwar couldn't stand the man and in the past had had to give in to his arrogance and disdain. He'd only met him over here in London but Hourieh had mentioned him back in Tehran. It had been one of the factors that Rebwar had used to convince Hourieh to come over. Her father had known Dr Gul's family. They were Persian and all pretended to have aristocratic heritages. Again, good marketing.

Rebwar smoked his cigarette while keeping an eye on

the office building. Lights flickered on in the streets and shops. The fashion boutiques glimmered and flickered their exclusive garments and accessories. Their prospective clients stopped for a look and at a reflection of themselves as if it was an assessment and check on their status. Rebwar saw Attesa walking towards him. He dropped his cigarette and surprised her by greeting her. She looked up, headphones murmuring some music and her eyes scanning him.

'Attesa, hi... Rebwar I visited Dr Norwin a few hours ago.'

She pulled out her white headphones. 'Yes... You'll have to call the office... It's closed now.'

'It's about my friend, Dr Gul. I'm looking for him. He's disappeared and I fear that he...' Rebwar breathed in and looked away.

Attesa looked at her watch. It was a gold Rolex. 'I've got an appointment. Can you call me tomorrow at the office?'

'Can I buy you a coffee, drink? My wife is missing too. You knew Hourieh... She worked there.' Rebwar watched her brown eyes darting around as if they were being watched. 'Just a few minutes, any information can help.'

'Who are you?'

'Mr Ghorbani, Hourieh's husband and I drive an Uber. Didn't she mention that?' He hoped Hourieh had said something about him. They hadn't talked for a while; Musa was their go-between. 'And Musa my son?'

'OK, but...' She looked around and sighed. 'She was your wife? But...'

———

The bar was busy with suited men and women. There were a few more casually dressed but they stuck out and either worked there or in one of the local boutiques. Attesa and Rebwar had found a seat in a corner. She had a large white wine and Rebwar had gone for a half of lager.

'When was the last time you saw Dr Gul?'

She sipped her drink. 'Must be a couple of months ago.'

'You must have a date? You keep all their diaries and...'

Attesa took out her phone and tapped the screen.

Rebwar sipped his larger. 'It must have been... difficult? It wasn't amicable, was it? What happened? Stealing? And was my wife involved?'

She drank some more of her wine and flicked her hair off her shoulders. 'She was fired first. Misconduct or something like that. He was... they were going through a tricky time. Lawsuits and...' She drank some more.

'When was this?'

'August. Musa is a nice kid.'

'Was he there too?'

'Yeah, school holidays I had to look after him. He helped out. Cracks me up with his funny T-shirts. Said you were a... copper back in Iran and a soldier. You know if it wasn't for the career I wouldn't be there.'

'You want to be a surgeon?'

'Oh yeah, love it. Nip and Tuck. The show?'

Rebwar shook his head. 'All that blood... does it not bother you?'

'Blood? Oh, it's OK. I help out. You know for those special clients. I know I'm not supposed to say but Musa knows so, hey...'

Rebwar hadn't known that Hourieh had taken Musa for some work experience. The thought of Dr Gul being some sort of father figure irked him. What had he said to him? Rebwar finished his lager. 'Was she sleeping with him?'

'Who? You mean... Yes.'

Rebwar got up knocking over the chair. The metallic bang startled the crowd who turned to him. They quickly returned to their conversations. 'Want another?'

'Sorry... He's... a shit. No one really liked him. And, yes, the same please.'

Rebwar saw her embarrassment. She was picking her nails. He went over to order. This time it was brandy, which he downed as soon as it came, and a pint of lager with a large Pinot Grigio. He didn't see much from back from the twenty-pound note.

'OK, so what was Dr Gul up to? Opioids? You know he's been found. Dead in a sewer with opioids.'

'No! You're shitting me. Sweet baby Jesus!' Attesa gulped her wine and leaned back in her seat for support. 'Why?'

'I'd like to know that too.'

'Why are you only telling me now? You... you knew this. You're playing games.'

'I need to know.'

'And the police? Why haven't they come to us and...' Attesa stared at Rebwar.

'Look, Attesa, they know about it and are...' He sighed. 'It's under investigation.'

'Musa was right. You are an undercover cop. I thought he was trying to make himself interesting. I joked about it. And he got upset. Fuck!'

'What did Dr Gul say?'

Attesa picked her phone off the table and tapped. Rebwar grabbed it off her.

'Hey, what the fuck! You—'

'Attesa, listen to me. Listen to me carefully. Someone killed Dr Gul, which means there is a killer out there. Understand? Now I need to know what happened in that practice. I'm sure it's all fine, but I need to know that. And I need to find my family.'

'You knew all this time. How could you play me? No!'

Rebwar felt for his cigarettes. 'I'm sorry, I just needed to know that you weren't the killer.'

Attesa's gaze froze, her left hand slightly shaking until she rested it on the table.

'Smoke?'

ELEVEN

Outside the pub, Rebwar lit Attesa's cigarette. Her pretty face glowed in the soft light. She flicked her hair back and drew another puff. She stared at Rebwar and there was anger in her eyes.

'What happened at the practice?'

'They always argued. That's not a secret – even the clients knew that. They still do.'

'About what?'

'Money… clients… everything – I've stopped listening.'

Rebwar leaned against the pub's brick wall. There was a couple smoking on the corner. 'Did they know that Dr Gul was selling opioids on the black market?'

'Maybe. Like I said, I stopped listening a while ago. Probably why I've still got my job. You think one of them killed him?'

'Maybe, but I need to get in there,' Rebwar replied in a hushed voice. 'Can you help me?'

Attesa shivered. 'Oh my God. Where's the police? We need to call them. I can't just go in.'

Rebwar couldn't really tell her not to as she would

inevitably be worried. 'Can you let me in before you do that?'

———

Rebwar and Raj waited at Eat, a chain restaurant that mostly served lunch to the office crowd. It was a fusion of Asian and a sandwich shop. Raj had already ordered and was eating a hot and sour chicken pot with a cheese and onion pie. It was a step into the unknown for Raj who never ventured out of fast-food chains. But Attesa Maddox had called the meeting and said she wanted to meet there. It was dark outside on Regent Street and rush hour was dying down.

'Uncle, Uncle you should try it. It's good.' Raj looked behind him at the lit menu above the tills. 'I'll share with you...'

'Raj... again, no. We've got a job to do. OK?'

'Oh, don't be such a killjoy. We'll be in and out. Just get Attesa to agree...' Raj leaned in. 'She's cute, has she got a BF?'

Rebwar smiled. 'Sure you know.'

Raj shook his head. 'I... It says it's complicated. But lots of people use that. Kind of a joke... You know this isn't a serious place or not bothered to be here. My profile is all made up.'

Rebwar nodded as if he somehow understood. She was now twenty minutes late and he wanted to call her. 'You've got the computer?'

'Yeah, Uncle.' Raj slurped up his soup. 'Keep your knickers on, it'll be fine.'

Rebwar was desperate for a smoke and struggled to keep

himself seated. 'Did you find anything else? Amin? Khan-Win? Hourieh?'

Raj lifted the bucket and finished its contents.

Attesa Maddox walked in. Her hair was tied up and she had a huge white leather handbag over her right shoulder. Only her black jeans didn't match the rest of her clinical look. Rebwar stood up to greet her.

'Sorry, I'm late,' she said. 'Had a work call. Long story.'

Raj wiped his hand on the napkin. 'I'm Raj, sure he's mentioned me.'

Attesa looked over to Rebwar.

'An old family friend. He's helping me with the computers. Now, you OK with this?'

'Yeah, about—'

'Fancy a coffee or something else?'

'Juice, something healthy. Ginger shot?'

Rebwar motioned with his hand for Raj to go and get it. At which he giggled and walked off. 'We'll make sure that you won't be involved. Also, whatever we find we can use against them.'

'Can they pay for my PhD?'

'Sorry?'

'Studies, I want to be a doctor.'

Raj got back with a little bottle which he handed over to Attesa.

'Doctor of what?' said Raj.

'Surgeon. They owe me that.'

'You want them to pay?'

'I was promised...' She looked down.

Rebwar noticed her eyes well up. 'You OK?'

She sniffed.

'Did one of them...'

She nodded.

'You don't have to come with us. You just need to make a complaint.'

'No, no, it has to be me. You need my pass and they'll know – and I want them to know. I don't want to go in front of a jury and be judged. Don't wasn't people to know that I was abused. OK?' She looked up, her eyes staring fiercely at Raj and Rebwar. She undid the lid and drank the shot. Her face tightened.

'You OK?'

'Right, better than vodka. I want those bastards to know that I know and that you're after them. Shall we go?'

———

Attesa used her key card to let them into the KhanWin practice. They all knew they were on camera and that her getting them access wasn't going to be a mystery. But Rebwar's hunch had been right: she wanted revenge on them. The office atmosphere was toxic and there was probably plenty to use. Raj went straight over to the reception and switched on the computer.

'Where was Dr Gul's office?' said Rebwar.

Attesa walked off down the corridor and Rebwar followed her. The thick grey carpet muffled their footsteps. She opened the last door to an empty office. Apart from an umbrella, a hole punch, and a stapler, there was nothing else. Rebwar opened the white cupboards but they too had been wiped clean. 'Do you have an archive room or office supplies?'

Attesa led him out of the room. How long till one of the partners would check the CCTV? He was sure they could log in to check. In the storeroom were boxes of paper and office supplies. He looked around for anything out of the ordinary – an archive box, or a file. But nothing.

'What did Dr Gul have here?'

Attesa shrugged.

'When he left, what did he take?'

'I never noticed. They came one evening and the next morning it was all gone.'

'Can I see the other offices?'

Rebwar went into each partner's office. He took photos with his phone. When they got to Dr Khan's office, Attesa just stayed outside and watched Rebwar. 'You know, I think he's having an affair with Dr Gul's ex-wife.'

'Oh, is he?'

She looked away.

Rebwar opened a couple of the cupboards; they were filled with files. 'Are all these on the computer?'

She looked in. 'What year?'

'Nineties'

'Not sure.'

He closed the cupboard and carried on looking around and taking photos. 'You know you're going to have to tell me about him.'

'Why? He can rot in hell.'

'I need to clear him for murder and if you want to get some money out of him... did he beat you up or worse?'

Attesa stepped back and held the back of her neck with her left hand and then rubbed her bare forearms. She paced.

'Ms Boyd, tell me about her?'

'Llaria... A bit like me. Started out as a receptionist and is now the clinic manager and studying to be an anaesthetist nurse. She's Italian. Done well...'

'And you get along?'

'She keeps herself to herself. Shy, I think. Was a little upset about the whole Amin thing.'

'Really? Fell out?'

'Yeah, sort of, she's quiet.'

Rebwar headed out and into Dr Norwin's office. 'What about these two?'

'Edwin and Vivek... Like little boys each trying to outdo each other. Pervs really.' She opened one of the large white cupboard doors. Inside was a series of photos of bare-chested women. 'I've caught him wank to this...'

Rebwar shut the cupboard. 'Has he?'

Maddox shook her head.

He carried on looking over his desk and drawers. He picked out a picture that was in a drawer and showed it to Attesa.

She stepped closer. 'Jolly Sweeney. Model – ex-model. She committed suicide. Yeah, she was a client. Tits and teeth.'

Rebwar looked at the picture, a young, beautiful girl in a bikini posing with her arms above her head. It looked provocative. He put it into his pocket. 'Raj, how long?'

'Nearly done... got a drink? Coke or something?'

Rebwar walked out into the hallway and nodded to Attesa, who went off to the office kitchen. He carried on looking at the standard office furniture and touched the plants. He was surprised that they were plastic. They were making savings. In the waiting room were old magazines a couple of months out of date. He ran his finger along the window ledges and they were dusty. Raj was standing with his laptop in one hand and a bottle of Coke in the other.

'Let's go.'

TWELVE

Geraldine waited for the kettle to boil and looked at the view from the second-floor flat. It overlooked a car park and she watched people getting into their cars and going to work, others taking their kids to school. For a moment, she missed the idea of having a family, something to work for and build on. In her marriage, they had talked about kids, but she didn't want them – not with him – and she wasn't as ruthless as some of her gay friends who did. To her that would have been betrayal, when you knew that you weren't going to stick around. The kettle clicked to a stop. There were two empty mugs in front of her. She started opening cupboards and drawers, looking for the tea bags. She found a box of Poroxy; the same opioids that were found with Dr Gul. She slipped it into her dressing gown pocket and carried on looking for tea bags.

She pushed the bedroom door with her hip and walked in with two cups of tea. 'Becks, I've got tea for you.'

She could only see strands of dark hair on the pillow and duvet. She put the cups of tea on the side table and sat down on the bed. Hands appeared from under the bedding and searched for Geraldine. They slid under her dressing gown. Geraldine felt Beckie's warm, soft hands slide over her legs and belly. The night's pleasures rushed back to her mind. She had missed her. They just clicked like two opposing shapes. Becks murmured and moved closer to her. Her dressing gown slipped off and Becks kissed her deeply. Limbs and hands wriggled into each other bodies. A box hit the floor and a plastic container rolled along the wooden floor, its contents sounding like little pebbles. Becks looked over.

'Yeah, found them. Are you?'

Becks got up and picked them up. 'Research.'

'Really, I am supposed to believe that?' Geraldine put on the white dressing gown. 'You're an addict!'

'Oh, fuck off! Is that what you think of me? I'm clean. Been clean for nine months. And working! You know if you still think that I'm an addict, you can just fuck off. Is that what you coppers think of addicts and criminals? That's it we're labelled for life? Put in a box and locked up? I thought better of you.'

Geraldine went over to her and sat in front of her cross-legged. 'Sorry'

'You should be.'

'I worry about you and... I'm scared.'

'Trust me, babes. OK?'

Geraldine reached over to the Poroxy bottle and looked at it. Opened it up and took out a pill. 'So what does it do to you? It's a painkiller, what's all the fuss?'

'Gets into your brain and your body gets used to it and compensates. Like heroin, a basic natal feeling. For me...' Becks cried, her head slumping.

Geraldine put the pill back into the container and twisted the lid till it clicked. 'Can I take them?'

'No... I mean yes take them.'

Geraldine got up and went over to the bathroom and switched on the shower. She closed the door and sat on the toilet.

———

She opened the bathroom door to find two broken teacups with their contents spilt over the floor. Becks sat on the floor wrapped up in the duvet and was crying. Beckie's hands were shaking and Geraldine slid over and held them. 'When you take one, please tell me, I'm here to help. Remember, I lost a sister and I don't want to lose you. And if you keep lying to me...'

'What? Like that bitch you're seeing?' Becks brought out Geraldine's phone from under the cover.

'Fuck! We're...' She hadn't changed the PIN since they had been going steady. 'It's complicated. Look at us.'

'Is there an us? What was last night all about? Your investigation? As usual, use and abuse. I thought you cared about me. Fuck even loved me.'

'I do, Becks, but...'

What? I'm an addict?' Becks grabbed the Poroxy container and ran for the door.

'Becks, stop it! Don't!'

Beckie had opened it and had a handful of pills in her hands. 'I'm going to do it. I can't go on like this. Being used, lied to, talked to like I was some kind of criminal.'

'Please stop. You know that I love you. I just struggle seeing you like this. You need more help than I can give. OK? I've done wrong, been selfish. I'm sorry.' Tears ran down Geraldine's cheeks.

'Crocodile tears, you bitch. Why?' Becks' hands shook

and some of the pills fell onto the floor. 'I'm sorry, I'm sorry.' And she took a mouthful of pills and chewed them.

Geraldine ran over to her and grabbed the Poroxy bottle off her and with her other hand grabbed her jaw to stop her swallowing. Becks' eyes rolled back. Her body was going into shock.

THIRTEEN

It was 9:57 am and Rebwar had just rung the buzzer and was waiting for Bijan's imposing black gloss door. It had been a while since he'd seen him and he actually couldn't remember much about their last meeting. It was when Hourieh had left him. Bijan had given him a few too many whiskies, and he'd ended up sleeping on the couch. Even though Bijan had been a friend of Hourieh's father he had stuck by him and supported him. And for a corrupt exiled elite he considered him a friend. The door opened and Rebwar was greeted by a tall slender man wearing a black turban, and his beard was braided.

'I've come to see Bijan and I have an appointment.'

'Yes, sir. Can I ask who you are and what it's regarding?'

'Rebwar. And he knows.' Rebwar crushed out his cigarette with his foot.

He was made to wait in one of the many living rooms. This one faced the manicured back garden with its pool. The furniture was the usual white opulent sofas and shiny tables. Sculptures and paintings added some warmth to the room. He was sure they were famous and expensive, but he wasn't here to pry. Another man arrived with coffee; he was similarly dressed to the other: black suit with a grey striped waistcoat. Without a word, he placed it on one of the side tables and walked off. Rebwar poured himself a coffee and added a couple of sugar cubes. A cigarette would have made it perfect, but he restrained himself. He had a long list of questions for Bijan and the last time they met he was frail as wrapping tissue. And he was still hoping to get his fiancée back from Ukraine. The Home Office had walked into his wedding and arrested her before he could marry her. She was whisked off and repatriated to.

The door opened, which was followed by some shuffling. Rebwar looked up, Bijan's frame was thinner and he slouched. 'My friend, good to see you! Please, please sit. It makes me hurt every time someone stands up and tries to help me.'

Bijan's breathing was wheezy and his walk unsteady. He took the closest seat to the door. Rebwar poured a coffee for him.

'Soldier, soldier.' Bijan waved over to him. 'Over there.' And with his bent index finger, he pointed to a glass cabinet. 'The key is in that Chinese pot.'

Rebwar knew the routine, probably every room had some kind of spirit stored away and it was like a little game to him. Once Rebwar had freed the crystal decanter from its jail, he smelled its contents. It wasn't a vintage he recognised but was some exclusive whisky, he guessed. He poured two glasses.

'Cheers, my friend.' The two clinked their glasses. 'Fancy some pastries?' Before Rebwar could reply, Bijan had rung a little bell which he had in his jacket pocket. 'What brings you here?'

'Amin Gul.'

Bijan looked up and sighed.

'He's been found dead.'

Bijan shook his head. 'That man was trouble. Served in the army as a doctor. Saw horrible things... Like you saw. But he did well here and liked his women. Ahh, but he saved me with the blue pill.' Bijan giggled a bit, drank some of his whisky, and looked out onto the garden.

'Hourieh came to see you, didn't she?' Rebwar had to repeat the question.

'Yes, yes... How is she? You know you two are so good for each other... I...'

The same man who'd delivered the coffee came in with a selection of Persian pastries. Another highlight. Rebwar scanned them, eyeing up the Ghotab which were small almond and walnut filled crescent pasties. The man offered them over to Bijan who took two.

'Yes, she came here with Dr Gul... are they?'

Rebwar looked down and adjusted his black trousers. 'Yes, she worked with him at his practice.'

'Oh, I thought... Maybe I thought wrong.'

Rebwar sighed and held his anger. 'I think they were having an affair. Yes.'

'My nose doesn't lie. Are you a suspect?'

Rebwar lay back into the large leather sofa. He hadn't thought of that. Of course, he was. Was he being watched?

'You didn't do it, although I wouldn't have blamed you. He wasn't in a good place. Tried to blackmail me. The cheek! He owed me. I made him what he was. A good soldier. It was tough, but made men out of us!'

Rebwar tuned out. He'd hated that war, and any nostalgia made him angrier. But he knew that it was the trade-off; if he wanted something from Bijan he had to hear him out.

'And that charge... we surprised them all right. Those faces of fear. Ha.' Bijan tapped his empty glass.

'What did our friend Amin want?' Rebwar poured another round.

'Money. Always about money. He had some business that he was setting up. He wanted to export some medicine to Iran. Humanitarian reasons. And smuggle them in.'

'How?'

Bijan shrugged his shoulders and brushed back his few strands of hair.

'So he wanted money. And can I ask how he was he going to blackmail you?'

Bijan took the glass from Rebwar and held it with both hands. 'War stories – nothing he could prove. Nothing. He was trying it on, the coward. I had more on him... and...' He lifted his bent index finger. 'I didn't kill him or have him killed...' In a soft, concerned voice, he said. 'How did he die?'

'In a sewer.'

Bijan lifted his arms and let them drop onto his thighs. 'Like a rat. Well, it was his own doing. So, who killed him?'

Rebwar shrugged back.

'Hourieh? Don't underestimate women. You know what they say... Sure, our friend Amin wasn't too kind, but if he didn't get his way...' He waved his index finger.

'Have you seen Myrian?'

Bijan looked up. 'I have heard that she is still fighting that divorce. Money's gone.' He chuckled. 'And you, my friend, how are you?'

'I'm OK, my friend, OK. And how's Katarena?'

'Ahh, with lawyers. They are fighting. She wants me to go there but... Russians!' Bijan spat onto his thick carpet. 'I'd rather die in a sewer.'

'You know that I think Amin was smuggling and selling opioids. It's like heroin.'

'Stay away from that. Drugs. Bad people, bad people. They kill each other. I had friends that thought it was a good business but... got killed.' With a tilted head, he smiled.

Rebwar took out a cigarette and showed it to him. Bijan waved him to go outside.

———

Rebwar lit up on the large, tiled patio that overlooked the garden. He noticed the back of the kitchen to his left and saw the chef having a cigarette. He went over to him and greeted him. He was portly, short, and maybe from India. Rebwar held out his hand and introduced himself.

The man wiped his hands on his blue apron and held out his hand. 'Manish.'

'Didn't know Bijan liked his curries.'

'Oh, he like it. Not so hot but he like it. You know him?'

'An old friend, do you remember seeing a couple? Doctor and a middle-aged woman...'

Manish looked up dragging on his cigarette. Behind him was a man cleaning the floor with a mop. 'There was a man who came here. Tall, fancy suit. Wanted to smoke.'

Rebwar nodded and passed him another cigarette.

He placed it behind his ear. 'You...' His brown eyes fixed on Rebwar. 'Know him?'

'He owes me a few favours. Old friend from back home.' Rebwar noticed Manish look behind him at a shelf. 'Did they stay for dinner?'

Manish stubbed out his cigarette. 'I needed.' And he returned to the kitchen.

Rebwar stubbed his cigarette and walked into the kitchen. He passed the shelf that Manish was looking at. There were three cardboard boxes with a shipping label. Rebwar bent down to tie his shoelace. He noted the Poroxy Pharma company as the shipper, and it was addressed to Steve Buckham. The boxes were sealed. Rebwar waved Manish goodbye and returned to see Bijan.

FOURTEEN

Rebwar was sitting outside the Shishwasi – his office and where he had a tab with his friend Berker, one of the old boys – an Iraqi Kurd with a thick grey moustache, thinning hair and a strong square jaw. He came up and wiped the stainless steel table with a towel.

'Usual?'

Rebwar nodded and offered him a cigarette.

Berker took one, tucked it behind his ear and smiled, revealing a couple of gold teeth.

'You've been winning at the horses?'

'I'd never do that, just been lucky.' And he walked off into the restaurant. It was a local for many of the Middle-Eastern population and the area had been nicknamed 'Little Cairo.' It served the traditional mezze dishes of the region, kebabs, tagines and offered shish which people smoked outside. There were a couple of tables with groups of men sampling the flavoured tobaccos. Raj had managed to hack into Dr Gul's Facebook account and found some interesting info. One that had stood out for Rebwar was a wedding picture where a friend of his had been tagged: Dr

Issac Felber, who had been his best man. Rebwar wanted to know more and he had phoned him for a meeting.

Rebwar checked his watch; Dr Felber was late. Berker arrived with a coffee. He could sense he was looking for some conversation. 'Which horse was it?'

'Dominos.'

Rebwar sipped the sweet black coffee. 'Remind me not to play you. Was it a clean game?'

'I don't know what you're saying. Look if you need... you know. I can—'

'Thank you, my friend, but I have enough trouble. I guess the boss is back? Music is back to the classics.'

'Heard about your wife and son. Sorry about that. You deserved better.'

'Gossip making the rounds? What did you hear?'

'That she left you and took your son. Hey, Tamar came round last night.' Berker leaned in and looked around. 'If you need some.' And he winked. 'On the house, she said.' He smiled and shook his left hand.

Rebwar smiled back but felt embarrassed; it wasn't something he was comfortable with. Some of his previous police colleagues had abused their relationships and taken advantage. This was a line he didn't want to cross even though it wasn't in any official capacity. She was a beautiful friend who worked as a stripper and that's where it was going to remain. 'I'm OK, Berker, but thank you for your concern.' A man caught Rebwar's eye. He wore a black polo neck and a brown jacket with blue cords. He had grey medium-length hair, glasses, and a handsome face for mid-sixties. He raised his hand for Rebwar to see.

'Mr Ghorbani?'

'Call me Rebwar. Please sit. Dr Felber.'

He sat down opposite him.

'Berker...' Rebwar pointed at Dr Felber. 'Coffee?' He nodded and Rebwar indicated that he wanted another one too.

'So, what's so important that I had to meet you?'

Rebwar offered him a cigarette, which he declined. 'Are you going to tell me to give up?'

'I'm not consulting you.' He looked at his watch.

'Are you running a clock?'

'Sorry, habit.'

'How did you two meet?'

'Sorry, but before we start. Why?'

'He's been murdered.'

Rebwar watched his reaction. He sat back in his chair, looked around and shuffled to the edge of the chair, and leaned in. 'When? How? Why?'

'He was found in a sewer in one of those fatbergs.'

'The poor man. And you are police?'

'They have asked me to investigate. And me and Amin... Let's say our paths crossed.'

Berker arrived with the two coffees, which he put on the table and left. Rebwar liked that he knew when to be discreet.

Dr Felber sipped his coffee. 'That's terrible. What can I say? Do I need a solicitor?'

'No, no. I just need to know a little more about him. I hear you were his best man.'

Dr Felber exhaled and pushed his glasses back onto the bridge of his nose. 'We worked in the same hospital as junior doctors. And he got married and then we drifted apart. Especially since his divorce. Myrian, you know she had reasons to be bitter. He always had an eye for another. That's terrible news.' He brought out his phone.

'It's not public. They are still, you know, checking.'

'Do I need to identify him?'

Rebwar stubbed out his cigarette. 'No, no. What do you know about opioids?'

'Oh, yes, I heard rumours... is it true?'

'What?'

'That he, you know... dealt with them.' Rebwar nodded and Dr Felber clenched his fist. 'The idiot. It's related, isn't it? I know.'

'What are pill mills?'

'Well, it's really more of a US problem. Pharmacies that overprescribe them to the most unscrupulous clients. That's what you get with private healthcare.'

'Who was he selling to?'

'Amin?' Rebwar nodded and Dr Ferber looked around himself. 'You see, in the US, companies that make opioids can sell them legally to doctors and pharmacies and the more they sell the more money they get. It's known that patients get addicted and then when you take it away they just resort to heroin.'

Rebwar brought out another cigarette. 'Heard of Poroxy?'

'Yes. They manufacture it.'

'He had boxes of them.'

Dr Felber squinted and finished his coffee. 'Sure it's not a setup? You need to visit his former partners at his old practice. That didn't end on good terms.'

'And if I wanted to get some here in London. Where would I get some?'

'I don't know... I mean that would incriminate me. And I haven't got the foggiest. I'm a retired GP.'

Rebwar wondered for a moment how honest Dr Felber was being with him. 'Why would you prescribe this filth if doctors know it's bad for you?'

Dr Felber gave a little laugh. 'Because they lied to us. They said it wasn't addictive and you couldn't break down the pills to powder and distil the agent out of them. I mean... it's refined opium. Look... and this is off the record... I will deny this, but there is a place where Amin used to get his dope back in the day. A little newsagent just off King's Road. But you didn't hear it from me. OK?'

'My lips are sealed. Drink?'

Dr Felber shook his head.

FIFTEEN

Rebwar had asked Berker if he knew about the dope shop and he had scribbled an address for him on a paper napkin. It was a newsagent on the back of King's Road and it sold dope for the Persian community. As it was now being more and more tolerated and seen as a medicine, this wasn't a big secret. But Rebwar was curious about what else the owner had in stock or knew. The shop was traditional with its shelves of magazines, cards, sweets, milk and stationery. The cigarettes were behind the counter in a closed cabinet adorned with warnings. No children were allowed to be in the shop if the shutters were to be opened to access the tobacco. A typical government directive – Rebwar would have loved to have been in that meeting when they came up with that idea. The man behind the counter had a thick grey moustache and combed-back hair. It had a purple tinge to it. Rebwar greeted him in Persian. Which the man acknowledged.

'I'm looking for Hussein, heard he can get something extra for my shish,' said Rebwar

The man looked around his empty shop. 'Follow me.'

Rebwar slipped the twenty-pound note back into his pocket and followed through a small side door down a steep spiral staircase. In the small cellar was a glass counter and old musty boxes with some odd bits of dusty furniture. The man tugged a piece of string, which turned the lonesome lightbulb on.

'Rebwar, looking—'

'ID?'

Rebwar got out his wallet and handed over his driving licence. The man put on brown thick-rimmed glasses and inspected it. 'OK, Mr Ghorbani. How did you hear of this place?'

'Dr Gul. Amin Gul.'

'You like some dope for shish.' And he got out some small transparent zip-lock bags filled with different cannabis plants. Their distinct sweet smell seeped out. Rebwar took one and looked at it. He had to think hard for the last time he had tried it. Must have been when he was serving in the Iran-Iraq war. Drugs were practically prescribed and most of the career criminals got their taste and training for their future careers. Since then he had avoided it, although, right at that moment, he was tempted.

'How much for this one?'

'Forty.'

'And if I need something a little more... You know...'

The man shook his head.

'Amin told me that—'

'Amin not welcome here.'

'Look, Hussein, I'll put my cards on the table. I'll buy this and give you a little extra.' Rebwar put another ten on the table. 'I'm looking for Dr Gul and my wife and son.'

Hussein took the money and put it into his trouser pocket. 'You police or something, Rebwar?'

Rebwar nodded.

'I have heard of you. Former policeman. You worked in which district?'

'All of them, Criminal Investigation Police of NAJA.'

'They sent you here to look for Amin? Yeah, he tried to sell me drugs. I only deal in cannabis. The other… I keep away. Too much trouble. Understand.'

'If I was looking, do you know who?'

Hussein laughed and shook his head. 'Call yourself police? It's everywhere.'

'What was Amin selling?'

'Ahh, pills for pain. Many customers ask me for it. It's popular, but no this still the best.' Hussein held up one of the sachets.

'Did Amin come alone?'

'What's your wife called?'

'Hourieh.'

Hussein reached for a pack of cigarettes that was lying on a chair with an ashtray. He offered one to Rebwar, who was obliged. He lit Hussein's cigarette and then his. Hussein shook his head.

'But he came with a woman. Persian.'

'Client can't say. Sorry. So has Amin run off with your wife?'

Rebwar tensed up. The gossip was doing the rounds. What was Hourieh thinking? 'Amin is dead. Found in a sewer.'

'Yeah, I heard. And your name too.'

'So you were expecting me. So who was this woman with Amin? I will find out.'

'No. Not my business. Look, I have a busy shop.' Hussein stubbed out his cigarette in the ashtray which he passed over to Rebwar. As Hussein put his products away,

Rebwar dropped his lighter. He bent down and kicked it off towards some boxes. He mumbled in Persian how clumsy he was and stumbled over to knock over some of the cardboard parcels. He noticed that two were identical to the ones he had seen in Bijan's kitchen. He stacked them back.

Rebwar went back upstairs and closed the door behind him. There were two young boys waiting for Hussein. Their eyes looked bloodshot and they avoided eye contact. Rebwar looked up to see a couple of CCTV cameras. He'd have to find another way to look at the video. A woman with brown wavy hair walked in wearing big sunglasses. The big woollen collar of her coat was up and she was using it to hide her face. She walked past him like he wasn't there and went up to Hussein.

'Excuse me, but we were here first.'

The woman walked over to the back.

'We were here first,' said the other boy. 'Get in line, Mrs.'

The woman tried to open the back door to the cellar, but the catch had locked it. Hussein went over to her.

'Hey, did you hear me? We were—'

The other boy grabbed his hoodie and stopped his friend from going over to her. He protested for a moment but calmed down. Hussein opened the back door and they went downstairs.

'What are you looking at?' said one of the boys.

Rebwar's phone rang. It was Geraldine.

'She's in hospital...' Geraldine's muffled crying and breathing. 'She overdosed.'

'Who? My wife?'

'No, Beckie! You can be so selfish sometimes. Really. She did it in front of me.'

Rebwar walked out with the two boys staring at him.

SIXTEEN

King's College Hospital A&E department was full of people either seeking help or waiting for it. Geraldine was trying to make herself as comfortable as she could. She had been there for over three hours and it felt like a few days. The strip lights made the place feel like a lifeless pen where animals waited for their fate. It was a mix of drunks and DIY injuries with a few mystery cases. Worried faces stared at the various notices that were framed around the austere room. There was the odd fight with the broken food and drink dispenser. Geraldine tried to stop fiddling with her phone, which was about to run out of battery. Images of Beckie's face flashed. Her hands desperately grabbing her; sirens, tubes, flashing lights, faces asking her for information. Geraldine looked into the ceiling lights hoping for the mess to stop.

'Hey, how are you?'

Geraldine saw Rebwar's face and shook her head. Breathed in.

'Is she OK?'

She stood up and hugged Rebwar, tears running down

her cheeks; felt his strong arms squeeze her and it brought warmth, the kind she hadn't felt for a long time, not since her mother had died. She stepped back and wiped her tears.' She... She's in intensive care. Touch and go they said.'

'What happened?'

Feeling her body give in again, Geraldine sat down. 'Pills. She tried to... or might have killed herself.'

Rebwar crouched in front of her. 'Have you seen her?'

Geraldine shook her head again. 'She had a box of those opioids. You know... the ones that they found by Dr Gul's body. And... and...' More tears flowed.

'Can we see a doctor?'

'I don't know... It's all my fault. I... I should not have involved her. Should have kept away. Why? Fuck. Why?'

Rebwar stood up and went off.

Geraldine kept staring at the lino tiles, dull grey, scuffed, some of their edges peeling up. Sitting in front of her was an old lady holding onto her wooden walking stick. Big bulging eyes stared back through her silver-rimmed glasses.

'I'm waiting for my husband. He's been here since August.'

Geraldine heard some raised voices coming from a corridor. It was Rebwar. She went over to see. Rebwar had his hand stretched out onto the wall, holding back a male nurse.

'Rebs, what are you—"

'He's going to see her.

'How is she?'

'Can you please let me through? You will need to talk to the consultant. OK?'

Geraldine read the man's ID card. 'Mr Nowak, I'm her

next of kin. I need to see her. I came here with her and have now been waiting for over six hours. Do you understand...'

Novak looked down and tried to walk around them. Rebwar and Geraldine moved to block him.

'I am going to have to call security.'

Geraldine flashed her warrant card.

Novak walked in the other direction. They followed.

'Mr Novak, please help me. Where is she?'

'Security?'

And two men in stab vests came out from a side corridor. One was black and the other Asian. Both wore short sleeves and had tattoos on their arms.

'These two are stopping me from doing my job.'

Rebwar grabbed Novak to stop him from going.

'Hey, hey let him go,' said the black man. 'Sir, you stay back. The Asian man went for the handcuffs on his utility belt.

Geraldine held out her warrant card. 'Gentlemen, calm down. I need to know where Miss Beckie Webster is. OK?'

The Asian man took the warrant card off Geraldine. 'It's a fake, innit. Feels it.'

'Hey! Chocolate police.'

The two men turned to Geraldine and took in what she had just said.

'Say that again,' said the black man.

'You heard me. Give me my warrant card and tell me where Beckie is.'

'DS Smith – if that is really you...' The Asian man brought forward his cuffs. 'I am restraining you as you—'

Geraldine grabbed his handcuffs and before he could react had locked both his arms. The black man pushed Geraldine against the wall. And Rebwar knocked the back of his legs, which made him fall. Novak ran off. The Asian tried to reach the keys in his pockets. Geraldine kicked the black man who was on the floor.

———

Geraldine and Rebwar sat outside an intensive care unit, both holding ice packs. Geraldine had hers on her right eye which was throbbing and swelling. Rebwar was dabbing his right hand. Both looked at the blank empty corridor wall in front of them. Nurses and consultants walked by glancing at them.

'DS Smith?'

Geraldine looked next to her to see a young man with a neat side parting and wearing silver-rimmed glasses and green scrubs. 'Yes.'

'You're here for Mrs Webster?'

Geraldine nodded.

'OK, do you want to follow me?'

Geraldine got up and looked at Rebwar. She reached out with her hand and fought back her tears. She could feel her dry throat tingling.

'Are you sure?'

Tears rolled down her cheeks and she flicked her head towards the ICU unit. Beckie was connected to a host of machines. She wore a mask connected to a ventilator, which breathed rhythmically for her. Geraldine felt her knees give and held onto Rebwar's arm. He guided her to a chair and handed her a tissue from a box on a round table close to the window.

'DS Smith, she is coming in and out of consciousness and you can ask her questions if you like.' The consultant must have noticed their ice packs and her fragile state. 'Are you alright? I guess it's urgent.'

'Is she going to be OK?'

'Drug abusers are a tough lot. They put their bodies through hell and, to be honest, I can never say what their prognosis is. I'm always wrong. I'm surprised that she's not been handcuffed to the bed.'

'Sorry? What—'

Rebwar stepped in. 'She's her girlfriend. OK?'

The consultant looked down. 'Oh, I'm so sorry.' He looked through his notes on his clipboard. 'I... I didn't realise. So sorry. OK, well... And with your injuries I thought... you know.' He looked down and read some of the notes. 'OK, oh...' and glanced over at Beckie.

'Is it serious?' sniffled Geraldine.

'Dr Webster... She's been here before. Opioids.' The consultant breathed in. 'Yes, we are starting to see more and more of this. A growing menace. Why prescribe heroin for pain? Do you know how she got it?'

'Heroin? I thought it was Poroxy.'

'It's legal heroin, a synthetic version. Fentanyl is another favourite. I mean...' He laughed awkwardly and pushed back his glasses onto the bridge of his nose. 'What do they expect giving out heroin for pain? All started in America where it was given out for pain relief after an accident. And the body just adjusts and wants bigger and bigger doses.'

'But she went to rehab and...'

'Sorry... I... It's when medicine goes wrong.' The consultant went over to Beckie and with his clipboard in hand checked the machines.

Rebwar was flicking the lid of his cigarette packet.

'Is she alright? Is she going to live?' Geraldine went up to the bed and grabbed Beckie's hand. It felt lifeless, warm, but no response from Beckie. Geraldine interlocked her fingers with hers like they did when they wanted to say something special. They would look into each other's eyes and find each other. But there was nothing. The machine kept pumping air into her lungs. Her chest moving up and down. More tears came and she heard them drop on the bed.

'It stops them breathing, fentanyl. It stops the brain from telling the body that it has to breathe. She's lucky.'

Rebwar walked to the end of the bed. 'Poroxy... where do doctors get that from?'

The consultant turned to face Rebwar. 'They can't, I mean they can prescribe them and then the patient has to go to the pharmacy. Do you mean pill mills? Is that what you...'

Rebwar looked at him. Geraldine looked up and said. 'Pill mill?'

'It's an American practice where a dubious doctor will prescribe patients opioids. And they have hundreds of patients that go round with multiple prescriptions to different pharmacies and get drugs.'

'And it's happening here?'

'Probably. I guess with the NHS, there might be more checks. But sure it happens.'

'And a doctor having boxes of Poroxy... how does that happen?'

The consultant looked up and out towards the window. 'Samples maybe? Pharma companies do give out samples. But doling out a couple of boxes of Poroxy? That's like Christmas.' He smiled and stopped himself from laughing. 'Sorry, but you know what I mean. And, no, I don't self-medicate.'

'Do you know a Dr Amin Gul?'

'No, sorry. Should I?' The consultant looked at both of them. 'Is that her GP?'

'Can she talk?'

The consultant looked at Geraldine. 'I expect Beckie to wake up in the next few hours. And then we should know if there has been any lasting damage.'

Geraldine felt empty and let the information sink in. 'Lasting damage? What do you mean?'

'She did go into respiratory arrest and we induced a coma. At the moment we just can't say. She might be completely fine. Like I said... We don't know.' The consultant looked at his watch. 'She's in good hands. I need to continue my rounds. Nice meeting you, DS Smith and...' He shook their hands and left.

Geraldine sat back down onto the chair and stared at the array of monitors. After morgues she hated hospitals. Rebwar offered her a cigarette, which she declined, and he went off to smoke.

SEVENTEEN

Rebwar parked up at end of Markham Square in Chelsea. He was going to visit Myrian Gul, who was living down a long row of connected four-storey houses facing a shared garden square. They were all identical with first floor white facades topped with sand-coloured bricks. He walked up the steps to the gloss black door and rang the bell. Below him was a basement, and potted herbs and shrubs sat on the windowsills. The door opened. Myrian stood there not saying a word. Her long blonde hair hung over her dark blue Hollister hoodie. He noticed that only her left foot had been pedicured with bright red nail varnish. Her bloodshot eyes looked him up and down.

'Rebwar—'

'Oh, my God. Rebwar! You've come to see?' She held her nose like she was going to sneeze but tears rolled down her cheeks.

'You've heard?'

She nodded and waved him in. As he closed the door, she threw herself on him and cried. Rebwar hugged her. He could see himself in the huge mirror that hung in the long thin hallway. He felt awkward. He hardly knew her and couldn't remember the last time they met. She pulled away and Rebwar handed her a handkerchief. Myrian brought out her own embroidered one with the initials MG.

'So sorry, I heard yesterday. It's awful.' She turned and looked at herself. 'Oh, so sorry, I'm such a mess. I should really—'

'You look beautiful, Myrian. You always did.'

'Oh, thank you. You're too kind, but you know... I'll just be a minute. Go to the living room. I'll be back in just a sec.' And she ran off up the black carpeted stairs.

Rebwar walked over to the living room, which was at the back of the house. The two large sash windows overlooked the small garden and faced the back of another row of houses on a parallel street. The furniture was traditional with a set of green Chesterfield sofas. There were a couple of glass cabinets filled with silverware and crystal. Two bunches of flowers had already arrived. Rebwar went to check who had sent them. The first one was from a woman called Caroline. The note said, Sorry for your loss, must catch up soon for a large gin and tonic. Love Caroline xxx. The second card had the initial V with a drawing of a heart. Rebwar carried on inspecting the room. He went over to a bookcase where there were some framed photos. There were a couple of Amin and Myrian in happier times and some old black and white photos of a young boy. Rebwar looked at the back of the frame but found no name. He tried to open the flap that held the photo in the frame. It slipped out of his hands and fell to crash onto the wooden floor. The glass frame splintered into shards.

'Oh...' Myrian froze by the door of the living room. She

was wearing a white blouse that showed off her cleavage. She had put on some jewellery and make-up. She looked like he had imagined her when Amin had first described her all those years ago.

'Sorry, clumsy of me. Don't walk in. There's glass. Do you have a brush?' He picked up the frame and the picture, which had fallen out. Written on the back of the picture was Turan 2001. Myrian came back with a dustpan and brush. Rebwar cleaned up.

'Can I ask how you found out? I know it's a weird question, but I only just found out myself.'

'Oh, yes police came around last night.'

'What did they say?'

'That he was dead... sorry.' Myrian's head slumped and she wiped tears away.

'I'm sorry, Myrian. My police habit. Drink? Gin and tonic?'

'Oh yes, I'll make it. Do you want one?'

'Coffee if you have one.'

And she went off into the hallway. Rebwar watched her baggy faded ripped jeans which he guessed must have been the fashion. She had always been a trophy for Amin and it was something he hated about him. Like an object that you own. She deserved better. Myrian walked down the stairs and shouted over for Rebwar to follow her.

The basement was a spacious open-plan kitchen with a large patio at the back. There was an island in the middle with the gas cooker. Myrian opened up the Smeg fridge, got herself a can of Fever Tree tonic and prepared herself the drink. She made a Nescafe instant coffee for Rebwar. He had it black with three sugars. The kitchen was quite bare and he thought she mustn't cook much. He had noticed a couple of take-away containers and a Domino's Pizza in the fridge.

'How long has it been?' he asked.

'Been?' She took a large gulp from her drink.

'Since he left you?'

'Oh, let me think.' Myrian went over to a calendar that was hanging on a wall. She flicked back some months and stopped at February. 'Divorce was finalised on the sixth of Feb.' She sat on a barstool by the central island. 'Thanks for visiting. It was such a shock. Heart attack – who would have thought?'

'Is that what they said? I didn't know. Hourieh texted me.' He lied.

'Oh, I heard. I'm sorry. Sure it'll work out. How's Musa?'

Rebwar sipped his coffee. 'OK, I think, I don't see them. I don't know where she is.'

'Oh, really. Wasn't she working for Amin?'

'Yes, and I heard they were having an affair.'

Myrian's eyes widened and she finished her drink. 'That fuck!' She got up and poured herself a large measure of gin with a little tonic. 'Sorry, sorry...' She stretched out her hands on the countertop. 'I... what can I say? He's a fucker, a cunt, a lying whoring son of a bitch and...' She took another large gulp of her drink. 'Sorry that he fucked your wife. No! Why the hell I am always apologising for that cunt. He's dead.' And Myrian held her head and cried.

Rebwar waited, not too sure what she was actually feeling. Mostly shock, he thought. He went over to her and gave her a hug. He told her that he had to go and but that she should give him a call anytime.

Afterwards, he sat in his car and stared at Myrian's house.

He'd just scratched the surface of what had gone on between them. He rolled the window down and lit up. He was going to wait and see who was going to turn up at her front door. He had a sneaking suspicion that there was another significant person in her life. His phone rang and he picked up.

'I'm at Dr Gul's house...'

Geraldine had taken a pool car from work. Hers was at the garage, having failed its MOT and was being worked on. She had her mobile on her lap as there wasn't a phone holder. She was still working on admin at the Empress State Building in Earl's Court. Going from one menial job to another helping process orders and mandates, it suited her fine, as she could hide in a sea of desks on the open-plan floor. It also let her help out on Rebwar's cases. She had gotten access to Dr Gul's bank records and credit cards. There were crumbs, but enough for her to find some regular payments to a man called Barney Patel in Hayes, Uxbridge. From his records, he owned a couple of houses there. After some threats, the man admitted that he was renting a couple of his houses to some men who offered cash. But why Dr Gul had paid him via bank transfer, he couldn't say. Maybe he wasn't trying to hide his tracks.

Dr Gul's house was on Dawley Road opposite the DHL distribution centre next to Heathrow. There was a row of about ten or more semi-detached houses. His was the last in a series of small square sand-coloured brick houses. They were the basic two-up and two-down with a small tarmacked parking space in front. Following on were dirty white facade houses with brown plastic extensions, details that made them look older. Each one had the obligatory satellite dish. Geraldine parked the car in front of the house. Where Barney Patel waited in front. He was short, bald, and wore an ill-fitting black suit and a brown shirt. His smile revealed a couple of gold teeth.

'Hello, hello, pleased to meet you, DS Smith.' He slightly bowed and held out his hand.

Geraldine greeted him, tugged up her trousers and cricked her neck. 'So, it's empty?'

'Yes, he paid, or his bank. I had no idea. What happened to the poor man? He was very courteous and polite.'

'Accident, and ongoing investigation. Can you open up, please?'

Mr Patel got out a set of keys from his black trousers. He tried a few of them till the glass door opened. He pushed away a pile of post that had gathered behind the door letter-box. Geraldine picked up a few of the envelopes. Some were addressed to Dr Amin Gul. They carried on into the hallway. The air was stale and dusty with a slight whiff of chemicals. Geraldine shouted, is anyone home and identified herself as a police officer. In the living room was a three-piece sofa set, still with its plastic covers on. All round the room were old newspapers and brown cardboard boxes. Geraldine looked into one of them and found white packages branded Poroxy. She whistled.

'Drugs?' said Mr Patel.

'Yep, but legal ones well, sort of. If you know what I mean.'

'But he was a doctor.'

Geraldine checked some of the other boxes and found other brands. She walked over to the kitchen, which was at the back of the house facing the small overgrown garden. It was clean and looked unused. She opened the fridge, which just had some milk and a couple of beers and more medicine. 'Do you rent these furnished?'

'Oh, yes. My brother-in-law has a furniture business. You can buy anything you fancy. I make you a good price. Yes, yes, see this table? Good quality, very nice.'

Geraldine walked off and went upstairs where there were two bedrooms and a bathroom. In the back bedroom were a couple of opened suitcases with neatly folded clothes. On the bedside table was a notebook, which she opened. It was written in what she guessed was Iranian. She got her phone out and called Rebwar.

'I'm at Dr Gul's house…'

'Why didn't you tell me.'

'I had to act fast. Where are you?'

'I'm coming over. Text me the address.'

'Wait… Rebs… idiot.' And she passed the phone to Mr Patel. 'Text him the address.'

Geraldine went over to the wardrobe and opened it to find a set of neatly pressed suits, still covered in the dry cleaner's protective film. She checked the pockets of the ones that weren't wrapped. She found some receipts and loose change. Apart from the boxes of medicine, it was still slim pickings. His phone was missing.

'Do you have Dr Gul's telephone number?'

Mr Patel nodded.

'Call it.'

After a few rings, he bobbled his head from side to side. Geraldine went into the bathroom and there was the usual, Head & Shoulders, Molton & Brown soaps, Colgate, an electric toothbrush, Gillette razor and foam. There were some rings on a top shelf just out of sight. She tried one with a blue stone.

'Nice, Looks good on you.'

There were four different rings and she put them in her pocket. 'Did you rent out anything else to him?'

'No, madam, that is all. Was he bad man?'

'Who are the neighbours? Your tenants too?'

'No, no idea. I have never met them.'

———

By the time Rebwar had made it over, Geraldine had already tried to see if any of the neighbours had seen Dr Gul. But most of them were away working and the others hadn't noticed anything.

'Find something?' said Rebwar, getting out of his car, which he had parked next to Geraldine's.

She just shook her head. 'Apart from a shit load of boxes with various medicines, one being Poroxy.'

'Addressed to Steve Buckham?'

'Who?'

They both went inside where Mr Patel had rearranged the boxes and was taking photos of the room with his phone. 'Mr Patel... please leave everything as it is. It's a crime scene.'

'But I have to rent this, I can't just let it like this... You say crime scene? What? How?'

'Mr Patel. Yes, crime scene. We have to lock it down and process—'

'How long? I need to talk to your superior. Understand?'

Geraldine showed Mr Patel to the door and gave him her business card. 'I've found his notebook.'

'Your colleagues have told Myrian Gul that he died of a heart attack.'

'What... the... fuck? Who?'

Rebwar shrugged his shoulders.

'Why?'

Rebwar went over to the boxes and looked at the shipping address. 'I found these at Bijan Achmoud's place. Looks like he was putting them around. We need to find this Mr Buckham. He's not covering his tracks...'

'I know. Strange... So what does this say?' Geraldine handed him the black notebook.

Rebwar opened it up. 'Looks like a diary of some sort. I'll have a read of it.'

'And I found this jewellery.'

Rebwar picked up the ring that had the blue stone, 'Hourieh's.'

Geraldine couldn't find any words to say.

'I've heard she was having an affair with Dr Gul. This says a lot...'

'I'm sorry, Rebs. Where is she?'

Rebwar shrugged his shoulders. 'Hiding?'

NINETEEN

Rebwar was back home in his flatshare and sitting in the kitchen with an opened can of Foster's beer. He smoked and read through Amin's notebook. It wasn't the treasure trove that he was hoping for but Persian prose and poetry. It kind of made him sick as he probably wrote it for Hourieh and his long list of lovers. From the subject matter, he was a tortured artist and revealed an air of arrogance that Rebwar knew all too well. He closed the notebook and reached for his phone. Achmed walked into the kitchen whistling. He put down a carrier bag full of shopping.

'Not at work?' said Achmed, while putting the shopping in the cupboards.

'Day off, I'm on the weekend shift.'

'Missing the games? That sucks, man. We're having some friends over for the FA Cup. And some girls are coming later...' Achmed winked at him.

'Know anything about opioids?'

Achmed stepped back. 'Dope, yeah, MDA, maybe... opi what?'

Genny shuffled in in a green hoodie and just his boxer shorts.

'Man, you look like shit.'

'Did my back in. Got any painkillers.'

'Sorry no. Hey, Rebwar, do you have some of those opioids?'

Rebwar handed him a cigarette. 'The doctor I knew is dead... NHS?'

'Dead?' said Achmed 'What kind of shit doctor was he?' He took out two beers, one for him and handed the other to Genny. 'I'll roll one for you.' And Achmed sat on one of the kitchen chairs, opened a wooden box, and got to work.

Rebwar got up and said, 'I'll see what I can do. OK? Need to call the family.'

'When are we ever going to meet your wife? Have you made her up so we leave you alone?'

Rebwar smiled, left the kitchen, and went to his room – which was on the first floor next to the bathroom – the tiny room into which they had squeezed the mattress; it curled up at one end. Next to it were two suitcases and a pile of dirty washing. There was no furniture and just a ceiling light. There was a poster of Chelsea on one of the walls. His flatmates had given it to him to brighten the place. He thought they felt guilty. Rebwar sat down on the mattress and dialled Musa's number.

'Dad.'

'Hey, son. How are you?'

'Yeah, hanging.'

Rebwar could hear video game noises in the background. He recognised it as Grand Theft Auto as Genny played. 'Winning?'

'What do you want?'

'Not a good time? I can call back. But I have some questions for your mother...'

'She's not in.'

Rebwar just heard gunfire and swearing, followed by silence. 'Did you get him?'

'No... He's the boss... Dad...'

'Yeah, son.'

'Is Mum in trouble?'

Rebwar dragged on his cigarette. 'Why do you say that?'

'Dunno... just...'

'Has she talked to Amin?'

'Don't think so... Dinah came by. She still wants me to go back to work at that boutique.'

Rebwar laughed. 'Is it good money?'

'Look, Dad, I need to go.'

'Son, what T-shirt you got on?'

'Weird. And since when did you care about my clothes? It says...' There was a moment of silence as he probably checked. 'Do not read the next sentence. And in small text below, You little rebel.'

Rebwar laughed and lit another cigarette. 'Is your mother there? I really need to talk to her. It's important. It's to do with the police and Amin. Understand?'

'Dad, Mum says that what you say is all lies. You're just trying to get to us. She doesn't want to speak to you. I think she hates you.'

Rebwar sighed, 'Son...' He held back his mounting anger. 'Please pass on what I said. It's important, OK? I know that I haven't been a good husband and father. But...' Rebwar felt a wave of sadness pass over him like a cloud blocking the sun. 'I'm sorry. Really. Is school OK?'

'Yeah? Most of them are from other countries. Teacher is a dick.'

'Made some friends? You know that's important. Keep in touch with your old ones?'

'Sometimes… Dad, I miss you.'

'I know, son. Miss you too. If you like, I can take you to a game. I have friends here and they gave me a Chelsea poster.'

'Cool. Mum doesn't let me watch it. It's not fit for a boy like me.'

Rebwar stretched out his legs and leaned against the off-white wood chip wallpaper. 'Don't worry about that. You'll soon be a man and then you can do what you want. Got a nice view from your room?'

'Dad, I know what you're trying to do… I can't say where I am…'

'Really, I'm your father… I have rights. Don't you want to see me?' Rebwar placed his ashtray on his belly and rested the smouldering cigarette. 'Need money?'

'Yeah, but I don't want to get into trouble. Amin…'

'Amin!' Rebwar jolted up and his ashtray went flying across the small room. 'Shit!'

'What happened? Dad?'

Rebwar picked up the lit cigarette and stubbed it out in the now empty ashtray. 'Have you been seeing Amin? Did he buy you that game? What else did he tell you… You know he's dead. Yeah, dead. Murdered tell—' Rebwar realised that Musa had dropped the call. He tried to call back, but the phone just went to voicemail. Rebwar typed up a text saying how sorry he was for losing his temper. He sipped his Foster's and lay down, looking up at the empty ceiling.

TWENTY

Geraldine had taken the tube to London Bridge Station and walked to The Clink Prison Museum in Southwark. The route was a maze of cobbled alleys packed with tourists and pedestrian streets that were lined with coffee and restaurant chains. It had taken longer than she had planned as local tours crowded the historical attractions like the Golden Hind ship and the ruins of Winchester Palace. Geraldine tutted and excused herself, clinging on to her thinning patience. She was already late for her meeting as usual. She stopped in front of a sign showing the way down into the museum. It said Clink prisoners this way. She had called the meeting with Highclere, her current Plan B contact. He had chosen the venue, which wouldn't have been her choice and not one that she would have ever thought of visiting. It was a classic tourist trap.

She walked down to the bottom of the stairs where the ticket office was. A big black metal gate stopped the distracted from entering. Geraldine paid eight pounds for an adult ticket and walked in. The place was dark and lit with spotlights. The damp and the old dusty stone walls added to the decrepit dungeon feel. Families walked from one exhibit to another. Geraldine passed them, ignoring the different metal contraptions that were used for torture in prison. She wasn't sure if it all was some kind of sick joke or an education. She found Highclere looking into a glass cabinet with various metal and wooden objects that were used to restrain and injure victims. His black skin glistened under the spotlight. He wore a three-piece navy pinstriped suit, white shirt, and white silk tie. He twisted his head and smiled at her. His immaculate white teeth highlighted by a spotlight. He wore large dark sunglasses.

'Welcome.'

Geraldine walked to face him across from the waist-high cabinet.

'Late…' He tapped the large-faced watch clasped around his prosthetic hand. He let a group of teenagers pass by before saying. 'Fascinating, don't you think? The ingenuity we used to keep people captive.'

Geraldine looked behind him to where there were four plastic heads stuck on spikes. The teenagers posed in front for selfies. 'We've got a problem.'

'And that would be?'

'I think the police are investigating Dr Gul's death.'

Highclere walked off towards the following room. 'And what makes you say that?'

'Dr Gul's wife had a visit from the police informing her that her ex-husband had died of a heart attack.'

'Did you approach them about this?' Highclere looked at the spiked heads. Their comical appearance made them look like cheap Halloween decorations. 'Who were they?'

'That's what I've come to ask you. You told me that it was a hush-hush case, of no public interest.'

Highclere nodded and walked off with his hands

behind his back. 'Are you sure it's not some kind of misunderstanding? I'm not going to wade into a bucket of shit, am I? Because there could be a really obvious answer to it. There generally is.'

'I don't see... Why?' Geraldine struggled to think what was so obvious about what had happened. 'You think they just got the wrong address?'

'Happens all the time. Dyslexic, or overworked, or just incompetence. Take your pick.' Highclere coughed and his sunglasses dipped off his nose to reveal a scar that ran off his left eye.

Geraldine looked away so as not to be caught staring. 'What are you saying? That I should just let it lie? It's upset Mrs Gul and what if... I mean, if she finds out that her husband was murdered, what then? People know...'

Highclere walked on and into a room with another glass cabinet and a figure of a priest kneeling and praying. 'I'm not going to report this on hearsay. I want facts, proof, evidence. I mean call me old fashioned but, DS Smith, do your job.'

Geraldine felt like taking one of the wooden mallets. 'OK... I'll carry on as instructed. Sir.'

'Now that's not what I said exactly, is it?' With his right hand, Highclere adjusted his mechanical hand and scratched the back of his neck. 'Find out what happened and report. But don't go in with your heavy boots and ruffle feathers. Just facts.'

TWENTY-ONE

Rebwar and Geraldine had driven out to an industrial park in Slough just outside London. Poroxy's warehouse was on Malton Avenue and Rebwar drove up to a set of grey gates. He wound down the car's window and pressed a little box with an intercom. He asked for Steve Buckham and the gates slid open. Rebwar found a parking space and then the reception. A white-haired man sat behind a desk, wearing bifocal glasses and a white shirt. Around them were a couple of TVs playing Poroxy advertisements and corporate messages. Geraldine flashed her badge.

'Like to talk to Mr Buckham.'

'Hello, officers. Yes, right away. Could I ask who is asking?'

'DS Smith and Rebwar.'

They found themselves in a meeting room with a large central table surrounded by six chairs and at one end a large whiteboard. Both sipped coffee. Rebwar checked out the biscuit selection. There weren't any he recognised.

'Oh yes, pass me the Jammie Dodger.'

Geraldine pointed at one of them and Rebwar picked a brown rectangular one.

'That's a bourbon. It's the round one with the red jam in the middle. Got to try it.'

Rebwar held the plate over and she took one. He looked at the selection. 'And this one?'

'Custard cream. Average. The Ford of biscuits. Try the chocolate digestives. That's a classic. Can't go wrong. That's the BMW.' Geraldine dipped her biscuit into her coffee and bit into it.

Rebwar followed suit and dipped the digestive into the coffee. Only half of it made it back.

Geraldine giggled. 'Schoolboy error, it's all in the dipping speed.'

The door opened and a pale, ginger, middle-aged man walked in. His round face smiled. He wore a black suit with a loose red tie. 'Hello, I'm Steve Buckham.'

They both got up and shook his hand and he sat down in front of the whiteboard. 'What can do for you?'

'Mr Buckham.'

'Steve, please.'

'Steve, we found some boxes and some of your products at a crime scene and we'd like to know how they got there.'

'Oh, well, I need to batch numbers in order to trace the route. It's all monitored and logged so shouldn't be a problem.'

'Why would your name be on the shipment?' Rebwar used a spoon to fish out the remains of his biscuit.

'Probably the sender?' Buckham held his smile, which showed a row of crooked teeth.

Rebwar shook his head and showed him a picture from his phone.

'I see, strange.'

'So how does it work?'

'What?'

'How does a doctor get himself boxes of Poroxy.'

'A doctor?' Buckham leaned back in his office chair. 'He doesn't. Unless they are samples. But that's packs, not boxes. We only ship to wholesalers and sometimes pharmacies and the NHS. And it's all tracked and monitored. Are you sure it was our product?'

Rebwar flicked to some more images of Dr Gul's house.

'Looks like ours. OK, another option is that it's been stolen.'

'Is that common?'

'Shrinkage.'

Both looked back at him.

'It's a line on our P&L. All industries have it. Growing problem as there is a demand for it.'

'Yes, so I hear. And I'm sure your PR department is working hard—'

Buckham leaned forward. 'Sorry, what's all this about? Do I need to get some legal advice?'

'Just some routine questions.'

'But a crime has been committed?'

'Like I said, routine and ongoing investigation. Married?'

'Uh, yes, and two children. Why?'

'Now, what amounts are we talking about?'

'Shrinkage? Yes, well, I'd have to look at my spreadsheet. Small percentage, part of the operating cost.'

'Do you try to recover it? Or alert us?'

'Like I said, happens everywhere. All businesses have a shrinkage policy. And, no, never had cause to ask for... Police.'

Rebwar picked out another biscuit. This time he went

for the bourbon and didn't bother dipping it. Its stale chocolate taste made his mouth dry. 'How much are we looking at here?'

Buckham counted the boxes. 'Couple of grand... Street value of about ten to twenty.'

'And that's OK? I mean that's a lot and there's more.'

'More?' Buckham undid his shirt's top button.

'Yes, and it's been sold on the black market. Does your boss know this?'

Buckham's brow had a shine to it. 'Oh, well, like I said, part of the operating cost. Unless it's an unusually large number, well... then we might take action. But in all my years here I haven't had to... to report it.'

'Well, Mr Buckham, could you find us all the tracking information? We need to find out how it got into this man's hands. As he wasn't supposed to have it. Do you think you could get it?'

'What, now?' Buckham looked up and checked his phone. 'I'm going to have to generate a report and double-check it. And make some phone calls. I'm afraid, end of play earliest. Sorry.'

'Can you email it to me?' Geraldine handed over her business card. 'ASAP. This is a murder investigation.'

'Gosh, murder.' Buckham picked up a glass of water and drank a slug. 'I see, OK, end of play.'

'As much detail as you can get. Drivers, routes, schedules, dates etc...'

Buckham got up and shook their hands. Rebwar felt his palms were hot and sticky. The glass door closed.

'Lying toad,' said Geraldine. 'He's unaware of his shrinkage or there is something going on. Need to keep an eye on him. And let's check his background. Sure there is a link with our doctor.'

Rebwar took another biscuit from the plate; it was the last Jammie Dodger.

'Hey, I had my eye on that one!'

'You snooze you lose.' Rebwar bit into it. Again, stale, with a sweet taste of strawberry.

TWENTY-TWO

Rebwar and Geraldine were down in the sewers where Dr Gul had been found. Both were in blue overalls, face masks, goggles and boots. Their torches lit the old brick tunnel, which was wide enough for a car to drive into. The flowing green river was pungent, filled with debris and rats. As they made their way upstream, they found smaller feeder tunnels. Rebwar admired its construction; he'd heard that it had been built a couple of centuries ago and each brick had been carefully positioned. They still didn't know how Dr Gul had made it into the sewer, so had decided to retrace his tragic end. From the post-mortem, he had died six days earlier and that night it had rained heavily, which meant he could have been washed down. The going was slow as the floor of the sewer was slippery and Rebwar felt like he was wading through a flooded muddy field. He'd learned to only breathe through his mask, a trick that pathologists used.

Geraldine stopped, and put her arm up; her torch had found a rag. She bent down and picked it up. Rebwar saw that it was a shirt that might once have been blue. The M&S label was still there.

'Would he shop there?' said Geraldine.

'Too cheap for him.'

'How would you tell?'

'His vanity would give it away.'

She put the shirt back where she had found it and they carried on. Ahead was a fork in the tunnel where it split it into two smaller sections. Geraldine stopped in front.

'From the map, one goes southeast and the other south. I don't want to stay here longer than I need to. You take the left.'

'Meet back here?' Rebwar pulled back the sleeves of his blue overalls to reveal his watch. 'Back at nine?'

Geraldine nodded, and she went off into the tunnel. Rebwar took a deep breath, which nearly made him choke, and walked off down the other. So as not to slip, he used his gloved hand to steady himself. As his torch lit the path ahead he could hear little shrieks and scurrying. Some of the rats were cat-sized. It didn't bother him too much as he had lived with plenty of them in the past. In the army, they used them as shooting practice and some of his colleagues got a taste for them. This part of the sewer twisted and turned, which disoriented him. He had no idea which street he was under. At each feeder tunnel, he shone his torch, looking for any clues. He checked his watch. It was time he should be turning back but he decided to check out the next two tunnels ahead.

There was a suitcase wedged in a corner. It was the wheelie type that you could carry on a flight. It was something a lot of business people used and he was under some large city offices. He crawled into the tunnel and dragged it out. Rats ran by him. The case was zipped up and felt laden. Its black plastic hard shell was dented. More rats passed him, and he noticed they were going downstream.

The water level had risen since he had last looked. The weather forecast had said a clear night. Rebwar grabbed the case's handle and went back down the sewer. The water was now flowing harder and pushing the back of his calves. Leaves, small twigs and rubbish passed him. He was now sure that up above him it was raining. He had to get out before he was swept away like Dr Gul had been. There were no handy fire exit signs here. Water filled his boots. He still hadn't learned to swim. It had been on his list since his last experience where Raj had to convince him to jump in a lake or be burned alive. Surprisingly, Raj was a certified lifeguard, something he would have never guessed.

Rebwar held onto the wall. The sewer sounded more of an angry river than a calm stream. Rats swam past him. A couple grabbed onto the case. Rebwar tried swinging it hoping they would let go. He struggled to keep his balance, the torch, and the case. Ahead, he saw another side tunnel and headed for it. Water was now up to his waist and pushing hard. He had to hold onto bricks. He threw the case over the ledge which was waist high. The rats ran into a corner. Rebwar lifted himself into the small tunnel. He shone the torch and saw that it was a dead end. He was stuck. The water was still rising and he could see it. Rebwar took off his mask and breathed in a couple of times, trying to calm his nerves and think straight unlike the panicking rats. He shone his torch up and down the main tunnel and saw them crawling into another side access just up from him. He grabbed the case and got back into the water. It was now chest high and he had to use all his strength to wade across to where the rats were escaping. Again he threw the case in, then climbed up on his hands and knees and felt one of the furry creature climb over him. He tried to grab one, but it just slipped by. They squealed and fought each other. One bit him. He swore and kicked another one off him. He got up and used his torch to see what was ahead. There was a shaft that led up and there was a metal ladder.

The water kept rising. He went to the ladder and with his torch could make out a manhole above him. The brick walls were wet and water dripped on his head. The climb was a long one especially hauling a suitcase in one hand. Below him, the water was rising. There was no turning back. He was hoping he could lift that metal manhole.

TWENTY-THREE

Geraldine had taken the north storm relief tunnel that led up to Hackney. She knew it wasn't ideal to separate from each other but they didn't have the manpower to do this properly. Her torch shone across the slow-moving pale green water ahead. From time to time the slow-moving water flickered and she ignored the thought that they were rats. The bricks had changed colour to a darker red. It probably had some significance and, if she remembered, she would look it up. She knew a little about the great stink, which referred to London before it had a sewer system. It amazed her to think that it was built in the Victorian era and, once finished, was hailed as one of the wonders of the world. It surprised her that it was still standing and being used. She arrived at a raised tunnel and shone her light into it. A few eyes reflected and quickly scurried off. She shivered and scratched her neck, feeling a wave of goose pimples along her arms. Swore at them and carried on.

Later, Geraldine stopped to listen as distant sounds of dripping and rats arguing came to her. The high squeaks travelled straight through her. She hadn't told Rebwar about her fear of them. Somehow, she thought he would have made fun of her. Like the elephant and the mouse. The image made her chuckle – silly. She felt like whistling or singing and then shouting. She checked her watch. What had they said? Her torch picked up something red and she walked towards it. There was an intersection ahead. One end came from the city and the other went towards West Ham. If she hadn't got lost. The only map she had was a photo on her phone which was of a napkin. The Thames Water engineer had drawn where he thought Dr Gul could have been swept from. She checked it.

A deflated red balloon was stuck on the corner of the two intersecting sewers. It made her wonder how it could have got there intact. It was surreal. She carried on north although there was a possibility that he could have come from the city. She returned and shone her torch towards that direction. Again the brickwork was different: two tones, sandy and red. She checked the map again. This was hopeless. It felt like a goose chase that could go on and on. They didn't even know why Dr Gul had gone into the sewer in the first place. She decided to see if there was anything down the other tunnel. There were more muffled noises coming from that end. The water was also flowing a little faster, with the odd crisp packet floating by. She guessed the discarded chicken bones you found in the East End had been taken by her rat friends.

Ahead, a bunch of rats fought over something. Was this the break? She reluctantly walked closer to them. The beam of light didn't seem to bother them. All the others had just hidden as soon as she waved it at them. There was something that was worth fighting over. Her instincts were telling her to turn and walk away or at most call it in. She stopped and tried to see what was under the moving carpet of wet fur. Their shrieks and hectic movements got more intense the closer she got to them. By the water's edge, she saw some ripped jeans. It looked like there was something inside them, swollen, as the denim was taut and stretched. Her heart beat faster and her breathing became erratic. She looked around for a stick. She walked up the slight incline towards the edge of the tunnel. A huge rat was eating a finger.

She felt her stomach lurch and held herself to the wall, waiting for an idea to come to her. All of a sudden the rats stopped and looked over in one direction. It was towards the city where the noise had been coming from. Their shrieking died down. A couple of them tentatively fled off downstream which triggered a mischief of rats to bolt off. Geraldine stared at the half-eaten corpse. Its eyes were missing, and teeth and jawbone were exposed beneath a braided goatee. The body was partially clothed with bits ripped off. She was frozen. None of her training kicked in. The water rose around the body, which made its limbs move about. She had checked the weather and took out her phone in the vain hope that it had found some reception; there was none. She could hear water rushing towards her. It was as she had feared: a sudden downpour.

Geraldine looked around for a way out. There were access tunnels to manholes, but she hadn't thought of making a mental note of them. The smell of the rotting corpse hit her. Odd, she thought, why hadn't she noticed it before. The rapidly rising water pushed the dead body past her. She carried making her way towards the intersection where she'd spotted the balloon. She had to get back to where they had come in which was south. The sound of flowing water drowned out every other sense. Fear rose with the water and she knew she had to make a call: find a refuge or swim down and end up in that fatberg. Her torch picked out a raised side tunnel and she hauled herself in. It looked like a dead end, but above was a ladder that led up to a manhole cover. But she knew that she couldn't push it up herself. As the Thames Water engineer had told her it was a two-man job without a cover lifter.

Behind her, the water was rising and its flow intensifying enough for the sound to resonate off the old brickwork. She had to get out of there. She jumped into the cold water, which now reached above her knees. The body passed her. It didn't make sense. She had taken a left and headed south and the other tunnel where she had found the body ran east. Was it the same one? Her light picked out ripped jeans, a checked shirt, swollen yellow flesh. The rats had distracted her, and she hadn't paid close attention. Now the corpse was face down and all she could remember was the missing eyes and exposed jawbone. Water pushed her along and it was now around her waist. She had to get out, but there were no obvious exits.

Her wellington boots slipped and she fell. She tried to stop herself from being dragged off towards the fatberg ahead. She couldn't see it but she knew it was still there. Her hands reached out, trying to grab anything that would stop her. But everything slipped. She was moving downstream. Her breath quickened, taking large gulps of air as if they were her last. She felt herself lose control. A disconnect between her mind and body. She kept trying to grab onto objects and cling to the torch as if it was her lifeline. She felt something and grabbed onto it. It was the body. She had a shoe in her hand. It had come off. She felt a hand around her waist and let go of the shoe. The arm felt soft and sponge-like. It made her gag. She pulled it and this made the rest of the body push into her back. It was as if it was trying to grab her. She kicked out and punched. It wasn't letting go.

TWENTY-FOUR

Geraldine felt her body being pulled. She kicked out harder and punched out. All she could think about was how Dr Gul ended up, stuck in that mass of fat. She couldn't let that happen, and not with a rotting corpse next to her. She fought harder but she was still being pulled, water rushing over her, struggling to breathe, having to take ever bigger breaths as she tired. Then she heard a voice. It made little sense. Was this how it ended? A bright light blinded her. She could still feel the water and she was breathing.

'Keep pulling, nearly there?'

Geraldine tried to make sense of what was happening but panic was still controlling her.

'Easy, easy. Geraldine, Geraldine. It's me. Mike Collins.'

All she could see was a black silhouette. The Grim Reaper or a dark angel? Hands grabbed her and pulled her out onto a concrete slab.

'We tried to call you.'

Geraldine threw up. The emotion was catching up with her.

'Give her space... Where is your colleague?'

She looked up and saw Collins, white hair escaping from his bright yellow hard hat, thin black moustache and a large, pointed nose. His black eyes waited for an answer.

'We haven't seen him. Was he with you?'

Geraldine breathed in and nodded.

'Come on, guys! There's still a man in there.'

'Was that his body?' asked a man behind him.

'No, no...' Geraldine tried to get up but couldn't find her footing. Collins helped her. 'That's a John Doe. Need to fish him out...'

Three men waited for her to say more.

Geraldine realised. 'We split at the first junction and he went east.'

'Towards the North Eastern?' said Collins.

'Yes, yes.'

'Right... you two look in the tunnel and us two... we'll pop the covers. Come on, lads, no time to waste.'

Geraldine emptied her wellington boots.

———

Geraldine and Collins were in the small Thames Water Ford Fiesta looking out for manhole covers along Old Montague Street, which ran parallel to Whitechapel Road. The wipers were on their maximum setting and rain hammered down onto the panels. Street, traffic, and car lights all reflected off the streaming water. Both of them struggled to look out. Collins slammed on his breaks. Geraldine felt the seatbelt hold her back. He stopped in front of a manhole cover and stepped out with a cam lift, a sturdy metal pole with a kink, a handle on one end and metal plate on the other. Collins went up to the cover and caught a hook that was attached to a chain that was in turn connected to the pole. He planted his foot to hold the pole in place and with both hands pulled the top half of the pole. The metal disc screeched off. Geraldine went up to the black hole and shone her torch down. Only bricks and a metal ladder with dark water at the bottom. Collins repositioned the cam lift and slid the metal cover back.

Collins used his radio to contact his colleagues. 'What's your status? Over.' Only crackling sounds came back and he repeated himself.

'Does it follow the road?'

Collins drove off. 'Yeah, but there's some access tunnels around here. He could have gone in them for shelter.' He took a left into a small alley then stopped by a parked car and got out. He swore. A parked car's left tyre was over the cover. He took out a spanner from his utility belt knelt down and banged the cover, listening for a reply. He banged it again then shook his head at Geraldine. They got back into the car and drove off.

The radio's speaker sounded out. 'Mike, are you there? Over.'

'Any news? Over.'

'Found a black case, over.'

Collins looked at Geraldine, she shrugged.

'Take it. Anything else? Over.'

'No, we're about to go up the North Eastern. It's raging down here. Not going to be safe for much longer. Over.'

'Do you need backup? Over.'

'Not yet, over and out.'

'Uniform, Oscar,' Collins ended his chat. And he honked his horn.

'How many access points are there?'

'We'll find him. We haven't lost a man... not on my watch.'

Geraldine wanted to call it in. There were only three men, and it was only a matter of time till they had to stop. The rain wasn't letting up. Her fingers drummed the car's plastic facia.

Collins stopped the car. It was the same situation: a van parked over the cover. He crawled under the van and tapped the manhole with his spanner. He tapped again. Geraldine saw him wave her over and she jumped out of the car.

'Listen...' Collins tapped the cast-iron disc again.

As the rain bounced off the pavements, Geraldine leaned closer and felt the wet metal. There was a faint vibration. 'How are we—'

Collins had jumped up and with his spanner smashed the white van's driver window. The alarm went off. Lights flashed and a painful siren filled the road. People stared but soon carried on walking to find shelter from the downpour. Collins opened the door. 'Thank God it's a manual... We're going to push it.'

Geraldine and Collins leaned with their backs to the rear doors and pushed. The van moved slowly forward. People either ignored them or took a photo of them. Once they had moved the van far enough, Collins used his cam lift to open the manhole. Rebwar's head popped out.

'Oh thank God, are you alright?' said Geraldine.

'What took you so long? Cigarette?'

'Oh, fuck off.'

'English weather, we should—'

'Guys, let's wrap this up. Need to call in my team.' Collins closed the manhole.

'So, what did you find?' said Rebwar.
'Another body. And you?'
'A case, but I lost it again. We'll need to—'
'My men have it. Come on let's pick them up.'

TWENTY-FIVE

Rebwar was smoking and walking to The Dog House pub to meet up with Geraldine. It was on the corner of Kennington Road and Kennington Lane. They had met there a couple of years before. He'd had to rescue her from herself. He saw her sitting on one of the outside benches. It looked different to the last time Rebwar had seen it. The lower half of the facade and window frames had been painted bright red. The building's distinct triangular shape made it an icon. Geraldine was smiling and had two black pints in front of her.

'I thought you'd been barred from here?'

Geraldine looked up squinting into the sun. 'New owners. Got you a pint.'

Rebwar didn't want to be rude and ask for a lager. He sat down. 'You know I prefer—'

'All right then, I'll have it.'

Rebwar took the pint. 'Cheers.'

They clinked glasses, 'You can be so fussy...' She sipped the Guinness. 'They can't find that missing body. It might turn up in the Thames. Did you know that the sewer overrun tunnels go into the river?'

Rebwar shook his head. The sun had brought out all the locals and people were looking for places to sit. They had spread themselves to take up all four spaces. Geraldine had her legs up across the bench and was leaning against the pub wall.

'Fuck knows how that body didn't get stuck in that fatberg. I nearly did.' Geraldine shivered. 'We need to find him. I reckon he was part of Dr Gul's gang or one of his suppliers.'

'There were a couple of Poroxy boxes in that case I lost.'

She stubbed out her cigarette in the ashtray. 'The Thames Water lot delivered it to me and I got those numbers from Buckham at Poroxy. A lot of BS if you ask me, none of those numbers matched and we need to put pressure on him.'

Rebwar offered a cigarette and lit one for himself. 'What about if I get a job there? Security or delivery?'

Geraldine looked at him for a moment and nodded. 'That's a cracking idea and that'll make him sweat. What about the KhanWin clinic?'

'How's Beckie... sorry I forgot.'

Geraldine stretched out her legs and ran her hands through her brown hair. 'OK, thanks for asking. Hoping to get her out of ICU. And then we'll see. Sorry, I don't want to think about it. And that plastic clinic?'

'We need to put pressure on. I reckon they've had disagreements with Dr Gul and knew what he was up to. So they must know more. Can we question them?'

'You mean in a station? They'll lawyer up. How about we find some weak spots. Just need one to give in and they'll start ratting on each other. Otherwise, we'll be using your interview techniques...'

Rebwar knew what she was insinuating, his old school Iranian police methods were something he wasn't proud of. Plan B had forced him to use them a couple of times and he wasn't too convinced about the results. 'Find anything about the other investigation?'

Geraldine sighed and looked up. 'I'm going to have to speak to my ex. Highclere thinks it was a cock-up. I don't. There's something... I just don't know what.'

'Isn't that going to cause trouble?'

'Fuck them. They offered the case to us. Then that's what we'll do. Oh, I've got something!' Geraldine reached into the pocket of her bomber jacket and took out an evidence bag.

Rebwar took it and looked at the rings. He recognised them immediately and opened the zip-locked bag. He took out the largest one, gold with a coin-like face, it was studded with small precious stones, a present he had given to Hourieh for her thirtieth birthday. Musa must have been six. He picked out another: five interlocked silver rings. Another present.

'Hourieh's?'

Rebwar nodded. 'Were they in that fatberg with Dr Gul?'

'Sorry... Is she?'

'Yeah, talked to Musa but...' Rebwar took one with a cluster of diamonds. '*Gendeh*[1]...Wedding band.' Rebwar stood up.

'Sit! You can't run off now...' Rebwar sighed and Geraldine smiled. 'Get me another drink.'

Rebwar went inside the pub and over to the wooden bar, which was full of people waiting to be served. He waited, trying to massage his pain. Why had he taken her rings? To pawn them off, probably. And the wedding ring? That had shocked him. He had worked so hard for it. Double shifts, two jobs, sleepless nights. For what? He had wanted to make her proud, and impress her father, who thought he was a good-for-nothing. Where had it gone so wrong? He ordered a pint of Guinness and a lager with a brandy, which he downed as soon as it was placed in front of him.

'Pre-loading?'

Rebwar looked over to his left at a smiling man and took the two pints.

'All right then, grumpy chops.' The man left the bar.

Geraldine had put on her sunglasses and was enjoying the sun. 'Cheers,' She took a large gulp of her beer. 'Do you think Dr Gul was running this racket? He was your mate—'

'He was a shit. Dirty motherfucker who—' Rebwar breathed in and straightened himself. 'I need to find my wife. She seems to be a suspect in this. All my friends think so... and me. You know I wouldn't put it past Dr Gul that he wanted to set me up... or Hourieh. Have you looked at his bank accounts?'

'Yeah, nothing unusual.'

'Swiss accounts?'

'Is that still a thing? I'll look. What about back in Iran?'

'He left when he was just a kid. Not much family left over there. His uncle was there and his parents too. All dead. He lost his brother back in Iran.'

'Cousins?'

'Maybe, I didn't know him that well. Hourieh did...'

'Sorry... But I need to ask. You think she'd been having an affair for a while?'

'I don't want to know... Myrian. I need to get her talking. How about you having a go? Show her some crime-scene pictures, that should get her talking. I think she thinks she got away with something.'

A glass smashed on the floor, and a man shouted out to another man. Neither backed down and, after a few swear words, the smaller one punched out.

'Ten pounds on the small guy.' Rebwar put a note on the table.

'Twenty on the big guy.'

They sat there watching the fight.

TWENTY-SIX

Rebwar was on King's Road in Chelsea and was looking for D's Bijou, which was Dinah's fashion boutique, where Musa had worked for a little while. He'd said to him that he hated it, having to listen to all these rich women moan about their miserable lives. Although he did let it slip that he had fancied some of them. Rebwar still struggled to come to terms with his son as a teenager. He still saw him as his little boy. Past the post office, the road kinked left, and he passed World's End Bookshop and glanced into the window. In the reflection, he saw D's Bijou, which was opposite, next to King's House.

In the shop window were three colourful dresses, all three had gold and silver accents that made them look expensive. Hourieh had mentioned that it was upmarket and he could never afford it, even with a discount. He'd worked out that it would be just over a month's salary. Sure, Dr Gul could have afforded it, and for a moment Rebwar wondered if he had bought her a dress. He flicked his cigarette into the gutter and crossed the road. Inside the small shop were rows of hanging dresses and little tables with accessories. It smelled of a strong floral perfume and some trendy music drummed away in the background.

A slim smiling brunette approached him. 'Hi, can I help you? Looking for something particular?'

'Hi. Is Dinah here?'

'Oh, she's out back. Can I help?' Her eyelashes flickered and she held her broad smile.

'I need to see her, it's about my wife.'

'A return?'

Rebwar looked at the back of the shop and walked towards it.

'Sorry, but you can't—'

'She knows who I am.' Rebwar pushed a white door into a hallway that led into a room full of cardboard boxes. Dinah was standing there in bra and panties holding up a blue dress. 'Sorry.' Rebwar looked down.

'Rebwar, what a surprise!' Dinah smiled and stood there enjoying Rebwar's embarrassment. She held up the dress. It's a fabulous fabric. Feel! I was just going to try it on.'

Rebwar backed out of the room.

'Oh, don't be a prude,' she laughed. 'Come, come.'

Rebwar waited. 'Dinah, I'll wait. I'm looking for Hourieh and Musa?'

'Haven't seen them for a while. Tried Amin?' A moment of silence. 'Sorry, sorry very inconsiderate of me.' She came out wearing the dress, which fitted her and made her look taller and slender. 'I...'

'Nice dress. Have you heard?'

'Yes. What a fucker! Sorry, but he's not very nice to me.'

'Wasn't.'

'What do you mean?'

'Dinah, you must have heard...'

She shook her head. 'I'm just... you know. Sorry, he was so young.'

'Oh no. He was murdered.'

Dinah's face froze.

'And I guess they're saying I did it, aren't they? Jealous husband?'

'No, no, my...' She crossed herself over her chest and held her hand there for a few breaths. 'Coffee?'

Rebwar nodded and felt a sadness in him.

'Aza, can you bring us two coffees strong with sugars?' Dinah held Rebwar's hand. 'No, I'm not. Really, he had it coming. Sure, it's another jealous man. I mean, I lost count of the women he'd slept with. And...' She held his hand on her heart again and took a deep breath. 'I'm not proud and it was a low point in my marriage.' She looked away. 'I did too. That rat, he tricked me, I was vulnerable, understand?'

Rebwar watched Aza walk in with the two coffees. They both sat on stools.

'Aza, you didn't hear that. OK? So yes it was a fling. What happened?'

'Hourieh?'

Dinah shrugged her shoulders and sipped her coffee.

'Are they with you?'

'She did come by when she left you, yes, but... we fell out over Amin. He wasn't good for her. He's not a... was not a good man. Bad things—'

'Drugs. Opioids. That's what he was dealing with and they killed him for it. Now Hourieh could be in danger. And I need to get to her – she knows too much.' Rebwar's hand shook at the thought of it. Seeing it like that, he now worried for her. 'You have to tell me everything. Where has she gone?'

'Well... I thought she moved into Amir's but I've no idea

where she is living. I mean, Myrian's got the house. Have you called Musa?'

'Yes,' Rebwar sighed. 'They seem safe but he won't tell me where they are and I don't want to freak him out.'

Dinah held her chest again. 'You have to, Rebwar, you have to. If they are in danger. Call the police.'

'I don't think she knew what she got herself into. She had no idea. But I need to find them. And I know if she really was in danger she would call me...' Rebwar realised that it was a mess and he felt a mess too; like he was slowly losing control. That there could be a killer out there looking for Hourieh. But his reassurance was that if he couldn't find her then they probably couldn't either.

Dinah held his hand. 'Rebwar, I'm sure she's OK. I can ask around. Look, I'm sure it was some jealous husband. Some old story that caught up with him. But you really should call the police.'

'They are already investigating.' This was another slightly reassuring thought but he was waiting for them to call him as he was probably on that suspect list and someone was going to blurt out his name.

'Look, how about dinner tonight? I'll cook. It'll take your mind off it. I'll try to call her and—'

'Tell her that she is in danger.'

'Are you sure? Won't she just stay in hiding?'

Rebwar was torn on what was the best way to get to Hourieh. 'Have you got my son's number? You could try and talk to him. He liked working here with you.'

Dinah nodded. 'Yes, he must be worried. You look tired. Come tonight OK?'

Rebwar got up and walked over to the door and turned. 'I'll give you a call. Thanks.'

Outside the boutique, he called Geraldine. 'Hey, we

need to find out what the other investigation knows. We need to find Hourieh. They could be in danger.'

'Why? You know something I don't?'

'Because she could be involved in all this and they could be after her.'

'Shit... You're right. I'll make some calls.'

Rebwar took out a cigarette and lit up. He swore to himself.

TWENTY-SEVEN

Geraldine was making herself a coffee in the kitchen just off the large open-plan office. She'd boiled the kettle and measured a spoonful of coffee from a Kenco jar.

'How can you stand that stuff?'

Geraldine turned around to see one of her colleagues. 'Tim, it's like getting a job here. First, you try to reject it, then complain, then finally realise that to comply is just the quickest way to retirement. And this is instant, as it says.'

Tim Carpenter was a thirty-something pencil pusher; balding, overweight and eternally single. There was a bet on that he was still a virgin. He liked to wear cheap Matalan suits and grey shirts with loud ties. Today's was a yellow paisley number. From what Geraldine could remember, even though he was in the next cubicle to hers, he was a support services administrator. He kept telling her what that was, but it kept going in one ear and out of the other.

'I'd rather stick needles in my eyes.' He took out a Nescafé sachet and poured it into his own mug, which had Policeman, because badass mother f*cker isn't a job title written on it.

'So... What's that?'

'Nescafé Gold Latte. Only one hundred per cent coffee beans—'

Geraldine snorted, got out a hip flask, winked and poured some into her coffee.

His eyes bulged as if he had seen a horrendous crime. 'What the... You can't.'

'It's the only way to drink this shit. That's the real trick.' Geraldine leaned back on the kitchen top. 'Tim, I need to find an open investigation. Got any contacts?' She shook the flask in front of him.

He took his precious mug away. 'Ask HR or something.'

'HR? Really? What about a central database?'

He slurped from his mug.

'Got any mates in the PPS?'

Tim shook his head.

'Yeah, forgot... you're Billy no mates...'

'Fuck off.' He walked off back to his desk.

Geraldine looked at her phone for any messages and heard someone shouting her name. She looked out of the kitchen area and saw a man in a brown tweed jacket with thinning blond hair and sharp blue eyes, which were a little too close for comfort. Across the open-plan office, eyes stared in her direction. He noticed and walked over.

'DC Smith?'

She nodded and sipped her strong black coffee.

'DS Hunter. Got a minute?'

'Met?'

'Can we sit somewhere?'

Geraldine looked around. You had to book meeting rooms and all the private offices were for superiors. 'Outside?'

'Let's talk and walk. DC Smith, I'm working the case

involving an Iranian national and I'd like to know why you're nosing around it.'

'Funny you should say that...'

'What's this place? And what are you doing here?'

'Admin and...'

Hunter stopped in a corridor. 'Who's your gov?'

Geraldine took a deep breath. She was on her back foot. She wasn't supposed to give anything away. She also knew that she couldn't lie for toffee. 'He's not here... So where's your gov?'

Hunter looked out of one of the windows overlooking Earl's Court. Below was a huge building site where the old exhibition hall once stood. They were re-developing it. 'This isn't how it works. I found your name with Thames Water after you snooped around my crime scene.'

'Did you find the second body?'

Hunter turned to face her and his blue eyes stared into hers. 'What?' He crossed his arms.

'There was a huge downpour and a body passed me.'

'Did you think of reporting it?'

Geraldine crossed her arms. 'I was working on my investigation.'

'And that is?'

Geraldine stepped back to let a colleague walk past. 'I can't say.'

Hunter breathed in and clicked his fingers. 'OK, let's start again. I need to know what you found.'

'Poroxy. Heard of them?'

'Yeah.' DS Hunter looked down the hall. 'Oh, I get it. Are you IPCC?'

Geraldine looked at him for a moment. She'd heard that Empress State Building had at one point been used by GCHQ and it wouldn't be too farfetched if the Independent Police Complaints Commission could have been or were using it too. 'I can't comment.'

DS Hunter looked up at the white ceiling. 'Of course... OK. Either you book me or stay off my patch. I've got enough on my plate.' He walked only to stop and face her. 'And if I ever see you again...' He took a deep breath and carried on down the hallway.

Now she knew who had the case, but she hadn't found out if Hourieh was in immediate danger. She had to find out who DS Hunter was. He obviously had something to hide. She returned to her desk to dig into his life. But there wasn't too much other than that he hadn't got far in his career. At thirty-four and a copper's son, he should have been a DI by now, maybe even a DCI. She dug a bit deeper and found that his dad had been killed in the line of duty. He was fifteen years old at the time and was found in the squad car crying. Hunter Sr had been gunned down in a drug dealer's house. They never found the killer or determined the motive. He was the last person who should have been running a drugs investigation she thought. She had to call Highclere to get some answers.

TWENTY-EIGHT

Rebwar had decided to follow Dinah, as he still didn't trust her. To him, she had been instrumental in Hourieh leaving him. She had convinced Hourieh that the grass was greener and gossiped and taunted her into a new life. He was going to see with his own eyes if she was hiding Hourieh. Rebwar waited in a trendy juice bar next door which was a novelty for him. It served a lot of healthy-sounding drinks and salads. Even the teas and coffees were organic. The decor was rustic and basic with metal and wooden surfaces to give it a purposeful and industrial look. The clientele were all slim and well dressed. He certainly felt out of place with his expensive espresso.

Around six thirty Aza left the boutique and caught a bus opposite. It was only a matter of time before Dinah came out. He didn't really see her as a workaholic and there was the possibility that she was going to go out for a drink. But if she was hiding Hourieh, she would probably go back to her flat. She also was going to be aware that she could be followed. But he was a step ahead as he'd made a note of an address in Gloucester Square that he had seen on a cardboard box that had been in the boutique's back room. He guessed that it was her home address.

Around ten minutes later, Dinah closed up the boutique and got a cab. Rebwar looked for a cab but by the time he found one, hers had disappeared up King's Road. He gave the address to the cabbie and let himself be driven, something that felt like a novelty. The man tried to make some conversation but Rebwar wasn't interested. He looked ahead, trying to spot the other cab. He called Geraldine.

'Did you find anything?' he asked.

'Yes and no.'

Rebwar sat back in his seat. 'Go on.'

'I've met DS Hunter or should I say he found me, but he's not giving me much. He's not happy that we are or I am – messing with his case. Also, he now thinks I'm internal affairs.'

'But nothing on Hourieh?'

'No, sorry. But I think we need to get you a job at Poroxy. There's something odd going on there. How's security guard sound?'

'But... OK. He's going to know?'

'Best way to rattle his cage, I'd say. You'll start the day after tomorrow. Get yourself a suit.' And she hung up.

Rebwar was left to wonder if it was a good idea. The cabbie arrived in front of a large white apartment block overlooking Gloucester Square. The street lights lit the tall bare trees around. He paid the driver and stepped out. There was a reception with a porter sitting by a desk. He noticed some window boxes running along the front of the property. Even though it was mid-November, they held a mix of winter flowers and shrubs. Rebwar went over to the last one, close to the next property, and made a flower arrangement. It was basic but had some colour to it. He went over to a bin to find a newspaper and used it to wrap around the bouquet.

He walked into the reception and flashed his arrangement to the porter. 'Come to see Dinah Sasani.'

The man looked at him and dialled a number on his desk phone. 'Who can I say is visiting?'

'Bijan Achmoud.'

The man relayed the information and he nodded.

'Flat fourteen, yeah?'

The man nodded again.

Rebwar went over to the lift. The spotlights lit the expensive marble walls and chrome details. He arrived in front of a white door with the number fourteen. He rang the doorbell. It opened to a smiling Dinah, who soon stepped back with a perplexed face. Rebwar presented the flowers.

'You've got to be kidding... Why didn't you just say it was you?'

'Just curious if Bijan had been here. How's Hourieh?'

'Like I told you, not here. You don't believe me, do you? Men, you're all the same.' She waved him in. 'You got these from outside. You know, I pay for those. Part of the maintenance fee, but nice to get some.' She laughed and kissed his cheek.

Rebwar felt a moment of warmth. Something he hadn't felt for a while. He looked around the spacious apartment. It was elegantly decorated with large sofas, a Persian rug with a coffee table, landscape pictures of Iran and an inbuilt bookcase. The large windows overlooked the little communal park. She walked off next door to the kitchen where she laid the flowers on the wooden counter.

'You know, I'm glad you're here.'

Rebwar heard her opening her fridge and the sound of glasses and plates. He looked around for any clues that anyone else was living there. He saw some boxes in a corner. They were similar to the ones in her boutique. 'I won't find any opioids in here?'

She walked in with a tray and put it on a coffee table. 'Rebwar, come and sit here.' There was a bottle of wine and two plates with snacks. He recognised some dates stuffed with feta and a cucumber dip with crisps. She crossed her legs and tapped the blue velvet seat cushion next to her. 'It's been a day.'

Rebwar went over to the window as she poured two glasses of white wine. 'Cheers.' She handed over a glass and clinked.

'So she's not here.'

'Go ahead and check. All open and I've nothing to hide.'

'What was Bijan doing here?'

She smiled. 'You're all jealous. Smoke?'

Rebwar took a cigarette and lit hers. 'And?'

'He recently came to get Katarena's wedding dress... as well as some extra ones.'

Rebwar sipped the wine, which was cool and had a flowery taste to it. 'What kind of dresses?'

'Some long flowing ones, evening ones. Latest season.'

'Who do you think they were for?'

Dinah leaned back and brushed her dark hair back. He noticed the black lacy bra that he had seen in the boutique. She caught him looking and smiled. 'I don't ask questions.'

'Size? Similar to...'

'Katarena's? Yes.'

'You think she's back?'

Dinah drew on her cigarette and blew. 'Could be sending her gifts, I don't know.'

Rebwar sat on a sofa opposite her.

'Do you miss her?'

He thought about it. Hourieh had hurt him and if he was being honest it had been a long time since they had loved each other. But they had gone through so much. He shrugged.

'You miss your son. He's a good boy. He's a bit like you and if he uses his head, he might be something one day.'

'So, did you visit Amin's office?'

'What? Did I get some work done?' She laughed and adjusted her blouse and looked down her bra. 'You can touch...' She lifted her left breast and she laughed again. 'Courtesy of my last ex-husband. He wanted it and I said yes.'

Rebwar admired them for a moment and realised that she was only a few years younger than Hourieh. 'So what happened with you and Hourieh?'

Dinah filled up her glass and topped up his. 'I wasn't in a good place when we first met. And I'm sorry that I influenced Hourieh. I know you hate me.' She looked up at Rebwar.

'I don't hate you...' Rebwar finished his cigarette and stubbed it out into the ashtray. 'You...'

Dinah got up and sat next to him putting her arm on the backrest behind him. 'It's OK, I know I've done bad things and I'm... like you. We have needs.'

Rebwar felt his guard fall, her dark eyes giving him comfort and warmth. 'Dinah, I...' She grabbed his face and kissed him. He felt his body give in and she straddled him and carried on kissing him.

TWENTY-NINE

Rebwar sat behind an office desk in a small Portakabin in an industrial park. He was wearing a dark suit and tie and a Poroxy lanyard. The name Amin Drucker was written on it. The window on his left faced over to a barrier that let traffic in and out of the facility. It was the same one they had visited to see Steve Buckham. Most of the traffic was employees, and they just let themselves in with their key cards. A few he had to check and call up. He still had mixed feelings about this idea. He wanted to carry on finding other leads. His phone rang and he picked up.

'Dinah.'

'Are you missing me?'

'Yes... Look—'

'You're not going to make it difficult. I'm worried about you and—'

'I'm at work and can't say where and when I'm coming back.'

'You know what I'm doing?'

Rebwar had heard the sounds of splashing water and her voice echoed.

'I'm in a bath... love for you to join me. I'm so lonely here...'

Rebwar's imagination ran with it and he felt powerless.

'I like it when you go silent. It's when you're losing control...'

'Dinah,' he snapped back. 'I am going to have to call you back.' And he dropped the call. He looked up to see a man looking at him.

'Yeah, mate, sorry to disturb... Got a delivery and need a signature.' The man pushed over a piece of paper.

'And you are?'

'Jim Jacobi.'

Rebwar looked at the smiling round face with thinning brown hair. He signed the delivery note. 'Who are you going to see?'

Jacobi hesitated. 'Steve... I mean Mr Buckham.'

'You know him?'

'No, why do you say that? I just deliver, mate. Don't shoot the messenger.' He took the paper back from Rebwar. 'Buzz us in, you're making a jam of things. New here?'

'Yes,' Rebwar sat back down and pressed the button for the barrier to go up. He watched the van go in and made a note of the number plate. A text arrived. It was a picture of Dinah in the bath. He sighed and wondered if this was going to be a problem. He'd heard various rumours about her, mostly that she was a bit of a gold digger. But he hadn't much of that, so what did she see in him? He sat back and watched cars and trucks coming in out of the gates. The door opened and Buckham stepped in.

'Hi, I'm Steve... heard you let Jim Jacobi in.'

'Yes. He was delivering some goods for you.'

'You're new, right?' Buckham stared at him. 'I've seen you before?'

'No, don't think so.' Rebwar wasn't going to jog his memory.

'Right, I could swear that... sorry, I'm not trying to sound off... you know. But... He said you quizzed him. He's a regular, right? So next time just let him in, OK?' He turned around and came back. 'I can sign the paperwork. Sure I haven't met you before? You a temp or something?'

'Something like that. So just let him in?'

'Yeah, mate. Wave him in.'

'What's he delivering?'

'Sorry?' Buckham stepped up to the desk.

'If someone asks me, what do I tell them.'

'Oh...' Buckham rubbed his face. 'None of their business. Just let him pass, OK?'

'Sure, sure, boss. Just got told to make notes on who comes in and out.' Rebwar turned an entry book towards him. 'See.'

'Well, you fill it in and sign it. It's your job, right?'

Rebwar nodded and Buckham walked out. He watched him pass the Portakabins and noticed he was on a call. Rebwar got a pack of cigarettes and walked around to the back of the hut. He could just about hear Buckham talking.

'Yeah, mate, all done... keep calm, I've dealt with it... yeah, yeah.'

Rebwar dragged on his cigarette before a truck honked and he returned to his post. Buckham noticed him. He called Geraldine.

'Rebs, how's it going?'

'I think you were right. Got a name and a van to check out. Buckham is on edge and I don't think he's recognised me.' Rebwar gave over the information.

'What's Highclere said about DS Hunter?'

'Nothing... he's a bit shit. But we've been here before.

Good work I'll keep you there for a few more days and see what happens.' She hung up.

Rebwar sat back into his chair and looked around the small bare office. A few health and safety posters stared back at him. In the corner was a coat stand with his black leather jacket and hi-viz vest. He felt his frustration mount and wanted to interview Buckham and Jacobi and see what they were hiding. A van honked. It was Jacobi asking to be let out. Rebwar waved him to come in. He heard a door slam and Jacobi stomped over to the Portakabin.

'What?'

'Sign please.'

'Sorry?'

'Sign please.'

Jacobi looked up and walked over, red faced. 'Didn't your boss tell you? Just buzz me through. He's dealing with the paperwork. Not your problem.'

Rebwar passed the entry book to him. 'You need to sign out. Regulations.'

'Such a jobsworth. You're going to be hearing from your boss and my boss. Wasting valuable time here.' Jacobi quickly signed.

'And this box.' Rebwar pointed to the notes section.

Jacobi looked at the book. 'What?'

'What were you delivering?'

'None of your f'ing business, mate.' Jacobi walked off back to his van.

Rebwar walked out after him.

'Come on, open the fucking gate!.'

He looked at the van. 'Can you open it?'

'You're fucking kidding me? No.'

'I have to check what comes in and out.'

'I'm calling your boss, mate. This is taking the piss.'

Rebwar tried to open the back door but it was locked.

'Steve, that jobsworth is wanting to know what I'm carrying... Hey, come here, boss wants to talk to you.'

Rebwar took the phone. 'Didn't I tell you to let him pass? You total moron.'

'It's in my job description. Take it up with HR. But it says that I need to make sure that every access and exit needs to be accounted for. And as I am new here I am familiarising myself with suppliers.' And he dropped the call.

'Could you please open the back?'

'You're kidding, right?' Jacobi got out of the van.

Rebwar shook his head. 'You're holding up traffic. Quick.'

Jacobi unlocked the back of the van and Rebwar looked in. There were about twenty brown boxes that looked very similar in size to the ones he had seen at Dr Gul's house. 'What is that?'

'Sorry?'

'Boxes.'

'Yes, exactly.'

'From here? I thought you were delivering.'

'Look, mate, this is none of your business.' Jacobi closed the back of the van, grabbed Rebwar's lanyard and ripped it off him. He went over to the gate and swiped the name badge over the keypad. The gate lifted and he got into the van and drove off.

THIRTY

Rebwar had tailed Buckham to his house in North Town, not far from Maidenhead. It was a semi-detached house in a housing estate where they were all pretty much identical brick boxes. Over the years, people had added touches like a door porch, garage conversion and a tarmac driveway. Buckham's house was original and he had left the car mounted on the kerb. For a moment, Rebwar thought about calling Geraldine to tell her what he was about to do, like he needed some authorisation, but decided against it. He looked at the cream facade, which only partly covered the red and beige bricks. The lights were on inside and he could see people moving around. He guessed it was Buckham's family.

He rang the doorbell. No sound came from it but there was some shuffling inside and a woman shouted for someone to go to the front door. Buckham opened it, and he stood there waiting for Rebwar to say something.

'Mr Buckham.'

'This my house. How did you find me?'

'Can we talk?'

'No. Make an appointment.'

'I think we need to talk about Dr Gul.'

Buckham looked behind him and then stepped forward. 'Who?'

'Dr Amin Gul, one of your clients.'

'Sorry.' Buckham held his forehead. 'No, no you're... sorry who are you?'

'Can we talk somewhere?'

'Look Mr...?'

Rebwar didn't reply.

'I'm calling the police.'

'Better talk to me first, Mr Buckham. I can help you. He's been murdered.'

Buckham let out a massive sigh and rubbed his face. 'Now, how do you know that?'

'Can we talk somewhere more private?'

Buckham looked up and held his hand up signalling for him to wait. Rebwar stepped up to the door and put his shoe by it in case Buckham wanted to close it. Buckham went inside. There were a few words that were out of earshot and then Buckham shouted Rebwar over. He led him into the back garden onto the patio in front of the kitchen. Each sat on a chair, Rebwar got two cigarettes out and offered one. Buckham took it.

'The shrinkage you talked about.'

Buckham's tense face changed to surprise. 'Fuck, you're that... Fucking hell. Sorry for my French. Copper?' His hand shook.

'Not exactly, but yes. I was surprised you didn't recognise me...'

'I'm terrible with faces. But why are you talking about shrinkage? I thought we sorted that out. And what are you doing spying on us? Is the company corrupt? I can assist in any way, officer.'

'Start by telling me how your operation works.'

'Well, we package opioids and ship them out to distributors who then—'

'Mr Buckham, your gang... Mr Jacobi and the others.'

Buckham moved in his chair and finished his cigarette. 'I don't know what you're talking about.'

'Jacobi left with about twenty boxes of opioids in his van. And he was supposed to be delivering goods to Poroxy.'

'Really? Well, there you have it. You've got your man... haven't you?'

'You know Jacobi is just going to give you up. I will find out. And all this...' Rebwar pointed at his house. 'Bye, bye. Understand?'

The doorbell rang and his wife shouted that she was going to get it. Buckham tried to look to see who it was and checked his phone. His wife shouted for him to come over. Rebwar took another cigarette, lit it and looked over the messy back garden with its discarded children's toys.

'Yes, officers, can you explain...'

Rebwar turned around to see a blond man with close-set eyes and buck teeth and an Asian woman dressed in a black trouser suit.

'DS Hunter and this is my colleague PCSO Chabra, and you are?'

Buckham was smiling and had his arms crossed. In the kitchen, his wife held onto her two kids, looking over, concerned.

'I'm working with DC Smith making some inquiries,' said Rebwar.

DS Hunter grunted. 'Yes, OK. Well... this is a little

awkward. We must have got our wires crossed here. Have you finished with Mr Buckham?'

PCSO Chabra looked up at DS Hunter. 'DS shouldn't we see some ID?'

'Good point, yes...'

Rebwar looked at him and waited.

'Well go on...'

'I'm a contractor and you're going to have to contact DC Smith. Call her.'

DS Hunter and PCSO Chabra looked at each other.

'He's a fraud,' said Buckham. 'Arrest him. Come on.'

'Sir, let us do our business here.'

'He's the guilty party,' Rebwar said. 'He's taking Poroxy opioids and selling them off to the black market. Just caught his colleague, Jim Jacobi, taking twenty boxes today. That's what is going on and they were selling to Dr Amin Gul.' For a moment Rebwar wanted to add Hourieh's name to the mix to see Hunter's reaction, but that would have put her in danger too.

DS Hunter looked at Buckham. His wife told the kids to go upstairs and came outside. 'What's all this about?'

'Mrs Buckham, please go back to your kids. We need to talk to your husband.'

Buckham grabbed his wife who looked awkward next to him.

'Are you going to tell me who you are?' said DS Hunter to Rebwar.

'Rebwar. Go on, ask him if he knows a Jim Jacobi or Dr Amin Gul?'

'Look, I'd like you to leave,' Buckham's wife said. 'If you're going to accuse my husband then arrest him. I am not happy with this. Please leave now.'

'Mrs Buckham, like I said, this is voluntary. And, yes, I

can do this at the police station but right now it is in your interest to cooperate with us. Do you know Dr Amin Gul?'

Buckham looked down and shook his head. 'No.'

'PCSO Chabra, can you call this number and talk to DC Smith and work out what's going on. Mr and Mrs Buckham are you aware of Dr Amin Gul's murder?'

'He just told me.'

'Didn't you tell Mrs Gul it was a heart attack?' said Rebwar.

DS Hunter turned to Rebwar. 'I'm leading this investigation. Now please either stay here as an observer or leave.'

PCSO Chabra was at the bottom of the garden on a call to Geraldine. He was sure she was going to come up with some explanations for her. Rebwar lit another cigarette.

'Mr Buckham, are you aware that your company has a considerable amount of opioids on the black market?'

'No.'

Rebwar shook his head.

PCSO Chabra walked back up the garden and said. 'Sir, he's been cleared to interview Mr Buckham.'

'This is awks,' said DS Hunter. 'I still want you to be quiet and we'll sort this out later. I'm the superior officer.'

'Right, and who are they?' Buckham pointed to PCSO Chabra and Rebwar.

'My colleagues. And I don't like the tone you are using. This is a serious matter. Where were you on the night of the twelfth of November?'

'Here at my house with my wife and children.'

'Have you been approached by anyone about the sale of opioids on the black market?'

'No, never.' His wife held him tighter.

'Have you got any vacation planned in the coming weeks?'

'No, I wish.' He smiled at his wife.

'Well don't book anything. Thank you for your time and sorry for the inconvenience.'

They were led out by Buckham who closed the door on them. Rebwar imagined Buckham's panic. Now they had to wait for him to come running and grass on his colleagues. He wanted to find Jacobi to put pressure on him.

'Rebwar, what the fuck is going on? I would really like to know. This is embarrassing, degrading and frankly unprofessional.' DS Hunter turned to PCSO Chabra. 'What did DC Smith say exactly?'

'Just that he was authorised to interview... She sounded... you know – like a copper. Sir, what—'

'You'll be hearing from me.' He pointed his finger at Rebwar. 'Whoever you are.'

Rebwar watched them get into an unmarked Vauxhall Astra and drive off.

THIRTY-ONE

Geraldine was lying in her bed smoking, something she had told herself never to do. But things had changed and things were complicated and she wanted things to change. She was walking on the threshold of her comfort zone, like she had done as a kid; walked on narrow brick walls, edges of canals, scaled up trees, anything to make her feel something else. And to make some change happen.

'Hey, hon, give me a drag.' Sandra was walking out of the bathroom with her half-open bathrobe.

Geraldine passed over her cigarette and Sandra took it. 'Did you like the band?'

Sandra shrugged and kissed Geraldine. 'Not into folk bands.'

'You should have said... and they're not folkie. They're trending.' Geraldine turned around to get another cigarette from her night table.

'Just wanted to see you.' Sandra kissed her neck. 'Arrest me...'

Geraldine smiled, grabbed her hand and secured it in a

handcuff on the metal bed. Took the other hand and did the same. 'Bitch... I'm taking you down.'

'Oh, fuck... me...'

Geraldine's phone went off and she recognised the number. She got off Sandra and picked it up. 'Yeah,' she dragged on her cigarette.

'I've got something you might want to see.'

'DS Hunter? And what might that be?'

'It's a surprise.'

Geraldine looked over to Sandra.

'Go on... Fuck—'

———

Geraldine listened carefully to the satnav's instructions. She was on Whurley Way just north of Maidenhead. She had to stop before a crowd of people and park her car. She walked up to the police tape and flashed her warrant card at the officer. Once let through, she carried on around the corner to find an ambulance, more police cars and a forensic team around a car. DS Hunter came up to her with a coffee in a polystyrene cup.

'Morning, DC Smith. Fancy a coffee?'

Geraldine looked at the grey liquid. 'I'll pass, thanks. So what's the news?'

'Steve Buckham, he's committed suicide.'

She looked at him, waiting for another comment. None came. 'Suspicious?'

'Depends if you believe in conspiracy theories.'

'Like the earth is flat?'

DS Hunter walked over to the car. She noticed that there was a rubber hose running from the tailpipe into a hole in the boot. Half of Buckham's face was squashed up like a piece of dough against the driver's window. Both eyes stared out. Geraldine looked away. 'Why is he still there?'

'Can't open the car.'

'What? You could have smashed it!'

'He's dead and it's a crime scene. I mean, who would take the time to drill a hole in the boot? It's a setup.'

'Who found it?'

'A neighbour and then the kids.'

'Fuck. And they didn't break in?'

DS Hunter shook his head.

'So you think this was a murder?'

He sipped his coffee.

'Have you picked up Mr Jacobi?'

'No, but we're investigating all avenues. Oh, they've picked up that body you saw.'

'Homeless. Is that what you're going to say?'

DS Hunter got his notepad out and flicked a few pages. 'Mike Hays, lives in Reading and drives a white van. Courier of some sort.'

'Could have been. It was dark and I didn't get time to ID him.'

'From post-mort, he's got Peroxy opioids in him and they think he must have died in that sewer. Did you kill him?'

Geraldine turned to him. 'DS Hunter where are you going with this?'

His smile gave off an odour of halitosis mixed with coffee. 'Just pulling your chain. I am going to have to you ask to go and speak to the wife and the kids.'

'Me?' Geraldine pointed at herself. 'No, way. I'm not even qualified. Get social in.'

'It's an order and a priority. I need to know where Jim Jacobi is, as you're so interested in him, and find out if she knows this Mike Hays. I don't have time to waste.'

'DS Hunter, you can't expect me to go in there, a; alone and b; without the proper training. What if she makes a complaint?'

'I'm going to get there first for your meddling with Rebwar. Now, if you want me to be a good boy, get in there.' DS Hunter looked around and waved at an officer down the road for him to come over. 'Now you know each other, PCSO Chabra will escort you into the house.'

———

Geraldine knew that DS Hunter was trying to incriminate her and get some leverage over her. Someone above him must have said something and it had upset him. Although she still didn't know why there were two separate lines of inquiry. Not that he knew that.

'Ma'am, shall we go in?' said PCSO Chabra.

Geraldine nodded, opened the small metal gate, and walked towards the door dreading every moment. This was something she hated and she respected social services for doing it so often. She was going in there like a bull in a china shop.

She sat in the living room with Mrs Buckham and her two children. Mrs Buckham was slim, with brown hair and light in complexion, but because she'd been crying she had bloodshot eyes and a red nose. Her two kids were on each side of her. The son was ten and the daughter seven. Geraldine avoided their eye contact. There were three cups of tea and some digestive biscuits. The room was basic with few ornaments and pictures. Nothing flash or expensive.

'Did your husband leave anything behind?'

'What?' Mrs Buckham blew her nose. 'Like a note? No.'

'I'm sorry for all these questions. I know it's...' Geraldine took a sip of her tea. 'Difficult. Jim Jacobi. Heard of him?'

'Yes, he's Steve's...' Tears ran down her cheeks. 'Sorry. He was his colleague or something. Didn't really know him. Drinking buddy, I think.'

'When did you last see him?'

'Oh, a couple of weeks ago... Oh, hang on he might have passed by last week.'

'Aware that they were up to something?'

'Uh, you think that...'

'Mrs Buckham, these are just questions to get a clearer picture of what happened.'

'It's the police that came by yesterday. That's what upset him. Never seen him act so strangely. Like he had seen a ghost or something.'

'Mike Hays... know him?'

'Mike... Yes. Steve played squash with him.'

'Got a number, address? We need to contact next of kin.'

'Yes, somewhere, yes. Actually, just take all this, take it.' And she covered her face and her two children hugged her. Geraldine was welling up too. She took Steve Buckham's mobile and his wallet. She had got enough out of Mrs Buckham and stood up. PCSO Chabra drank the rest of her tea and took another biscuit.

'Thank you and sorry to bother you, Mrs Buckham. I'll make my way out.'

Outside they were towing the car into a covered trailer with Buckham's face still resting against the window. She quickly closed the door and swore. 'Can't they cover the car?'

PCSO Chabra looked powerless and put her head down.

Geraldine was about to shout over to DS Hunter but thought better of it. He was on their case and looking for any excuse to make them look incompetent. She got back into her car and called Rebwar.

'I'm going to give you two addresses and you need to get there ASAP. That body I saw in the sewers is linked to the other two.'

THIRTY-TWO

Rebwar had arrived at the first address that Geraldine had sent, which was Jacobi's. He was hoping to catch him, but he had probably heard about Buckham's suicide and made a run for it. This was another seventies housing estate not much different to Buckham's. It was about an hour out west of London in a place called Winnersh. For a courier, it was in the right spot, just off the M4 motorway. His house, if you could call it that, was small and looked more like a converted garage with a side gate. Ivy had taken over and covered most of the building, including half the roof. It must have once belonged to one of the adjacent properties. He parked his car close by and went over to the wooden gate, which was high and blocked the view into the small garden. There was no buzzer or anything and he pushed the door. It gave way after a few jolts. Inside was an oil-stained tarmacked driveway which was large enough for a van and a couple of old tyres were propped against the fence.

The entrance to the house was to the left and had two small windows. There was no sign of a back garden, just more tarmac. He rang the doorbell and waited. No sounds or movement. He got out his trusty lock-picking set and in a matter of minutes was in the house. There wasn't much of it. About the size of a large one-bedroom flat. The kitchen was a mess of dirty pans, plates, glasses, newspapers, car parts and empty food packages. He went through into the living room which was much the same with an old couch, TV, and more car parts. He found a couple of empty Poroxy boxes and carried on into the bedroom where there was a sleeping bag on a mattress and empty beer cans. The place smelled of oil, damp and sweat.

Rebwar was frustrated to have missed Jacobi. He looked around for more clues, for a computer or an old phone, but all he could find were some paper notes with addresses. A van pulled up to the gate, its engine clonking to a stop. Rebwar hid behind the bedroom door and waited. The front door burst open and he heard the sound of heavy boots making their way into the kitchen. Rebwar recognised the voice; it was Jacobi, and he was swearing and stomping around. He slammed something that smashed. Rebwar looked for a weapon. He picked up the tyre lever by the end of the bed.

'Jim.'

Jacobi turned, stared at Rebwar and grabbed a chair. 'The security guard... You've come for your lanyard?'

'Buckham's dead and so's Hays. Did you kill them?'

'How do you know they're dead?'

'Sit and tell me.' Crowbar in hand, Rebwar pointed over at a seat. 'How do you know Dr Gul?'

'I can pay. Money – is that what you want?'

Rebwar shook his head.

'You want the drugs... I can get more. Sure, I can.' Jacobi put the chair down. He continued to pace as if he was thinking about something else.

'Jim… Jim listen to me. The police are looking for you. They suspect foul play with Buckham's death.'

'It wasn't me, I'm not carrying that. The idiot did it to himself. I mean, really? What was he thinking? What am I supposed to do now? Hey?'

'Jim, calm down. You need to tell me everything. Who's behind the operation?'

Jacobi walked into the living room looking for something. Rebwar went after him.

'Sit down.'

But Jacobi carried on taking cushions off the couches and pushing boxes and rubbish out of the way. Rebwar went over to stop him. Jacobi grabbed a tyre and threw it at him. He ducked and it hit the wall and bounced out of the way. Jacobi made a run for the kitchen. Rebwar swung the tyre lever into the back of his knee, which made him stumble and fall onto the kitchen table. Jacobi grabbed a kitchen knife from the counter.

'Stay away from me. I'm going to get in that van and drive away.'

Rebwar swung the lever at Jacobi but he moved out of the way. Rebwar just wanted to disarm him. Jacobi thrust the knife at him. Rebwar grabbed his wrist and twisted his arm behind his back, squeezing his wrist till the knife dropped. Rebwar grabbed the back of his jacket and pushed him onto the floor. He stepped on his hand. Jacobi groaned. Rebwar felt his breathing return. He grabbed Jacobi's hand, turned him over, and cable tied his wrists, followed by his ankles. Rebwar sat on one of the kitchen chairs.

'Is it just you three?'

Jacobi wriggled, trying to get out of his bindings.

'We will find out and it's going to be easier if you tell me.'

'How?'

'I can let you go.'

'Who are you working for?'

'That's not important. Right now you need to tell me some facts.'

Jacobi tried to crawl on the kitchen floor.

Rebwar slapped him. 'Jim, Jim I will find out.' He took out a pack of cigarettes and offered one. Jacobi nodded and Rebwar placed one in his mouth. 'Now who killed Dr Gul?'

'We don't know.'

'Did you deliver to him?'

'A couple of times.'

'Where?'

'At the practice and once at the dropoff.' Jacobi drew on his cigarette.

'And where was that?'

'A sewer hole around Old Street. He had a little tent... you know it looked like engineers were working.'

Rebwar tapped some ash into a tea mug. 'Who else worked with him?'

'Mate, where are you going with this? It wasn't us... What happened to Mike?'

'Not sure, but he was found in the same sewer as Dr Gul.'

'Fuck! Albanians?'

'Why do you say that?'

'Just a matter of time till someone found out. It was only meant to be pocket money.'

Rebwar studied Jacobi. His forehead was covered in beads of sweat and he couldn't give an honest look. There was something. 'Are you married?'

Jacobi laughed.

'Next of kin?'

Jacobi's face froze.

'I'm going to go.'

'What? No, no. Hey, mate, untie me! I can't stay here! Someone's going to...'

'Who's the boss?'

'Steve. It was Steve's idea and it was just us – no one else.'

'And Dr Gul was just a client? Who else?'

Jacobi shook his head. 'Just a few doctors, like I said. It was pocket money. Under the radar – nothing big.'

Rebwar grabbed his packet of cigarettes and headed to the front door.

'Mate, mate, let me go. You said... Hey!'

Rebwar returned to his car and drove off.

THIRTY-THREE

He stood in front of a coffee machine. Since Hourieh had left him he'd had to make his own coffee and used the easiest option, which was instant. He had got used to the bland taste. He opened some cupboards in the hope of finding a jar of Nescafé. It wasn't his kitchen and he had no idea where things were. He found some coffee pods but had never used them. He pressed some buttons on the machine and lights blinked.

'I'll do it.'

He felt Dinah in her dressing gown hugging him from behind. Rebwar felt conflicted.

'I can learn,' said Rebwar.

Dinah got to work on making coffee. He watched her light, happy movements and they made him smile. His first impression had been of an arrogant, self-obsessed, bitter divorcee. She tapped her ass and winked as she made coffee. He still felt guilty. What was he going to say to Musa?

'What's your day looking like?'

'I was going to talk to Myrian again.'

'Maybe don't mention me. She's such a gossip.' Dinah

looked at her bare feet, which were perfectly manicured with red varnish.

Rebwar smiled and passed over a cigarette, and she passed him an espresso cup. He leaned on the counter and sipped the warm black liquid. There was something he hadn't felt for a while. At ease and happy. Dinah came over and hugged him hard.

'You know, when I first met you in that car park, I thought you were a rude and bad man. But I still wanted you... But you have a good heart.' She leant on his chest and listened.

Rebwar stroked her soft black hair. 'How's your day?'

'How about a duvet day?'

'What is that?'

'We spend the whole day in bed.' Dinah went over to the coffee machine and made an espresso.

'I wish. But I need to earn money.'

'What, you get paid for snooping around and asking questions?' She passed him another cup of coffee.

'It's complicated but yes. You heard of Jolly Sweeney.'

'Yes, that poor model that died.'

'She was Amin's client. Raj found her in his database.'

'What? He killed her?'

'Don't think Amin is a killer.'

The doorbell rang and Dinah went over to the intercom. Rebwar heard a series of yeses. 'It's a DS Hunter coming up.'

Rebwar went into the bedroom to get himself some clothes.

Dinah opened the door, still wearing her dressing gown.

'Is Rebwar Ghorbani in?'

'Hello, Mr Policeman. Yes, he is.'

'May we come in?'

Rebwar went to the door.

'Mr Ghorbani, you interviewed Mr Buckham and Mr Jacobi without my authorisation. I am going to have to take you in under caution to the police station.'

'And what?'

'I need to formally interview you. Do you understand?'

Rebwar saw that there were another two uniformed officers next to him. Rebwar's phone buzzed in his pocket and he reached for it. The officers reached for the handcuffs. DS Hunter raised his hand to stop the officers. Musa was calling and Rebwar handed the phone over to Dinah. The two officers grabbed Rebwar and handcuffed him.

'Boys, is this necessary?' said Dinah. 'Get off him, he's innocent. I'll get my lawyer.'

'Dinah, Dinah, it's OK. Let them do their job. Take the call and tell Musa I'm OK and ask him where his mother is.'

Tears rolled down Dinah's cheeks and she hugged him.

'Come on, off him.'

'And call Geraldine. Her number is in the phone.'

And they escorted him out into the hallway.

THIRTY-FOUR

Rebwar was in an interview room in the West Hampstead Police Station. The room was small with light blue padded walls. There was a white table with a recording device and a red panic button by one of the chairs. Along the wall around the room ran a white plastic box that had plugs and switches. With no windows, it felt stuffy and intimidating. Rebwar played with his cigarette packet, tapping it on the table and sliding his fingers to the bottom and flipping it around. He'd been in plenty of interviews and been on both sides of the table. DS Hunter opened the door, accompanied by another officer.

'Mr Ghorbani, this is DC Caffey. She is going to be assisting me. Coffee, water?'

Rebwar remembered Geraldine saying how terrible the police coffee was and he passed. DC Caffey was a petite woman with long, flowing, dyed blonde hair, her dark roots showing. She had painted eyebrows, which gave her a stern demeanour. You felt she had fought to get to where she was. She had a file, which she laid in front of her.

'Am I being arrested?'

'No, Mr Ghorbani,' said DS Hunter. 'This is just an interview.'

'Do I need a lawyer?'

'That's up to you. But we see it more as a courtesy interview.' DS Hunter reached over the table, started the tape recorder, and stated the time, place, case number and who was there.

'And you don't seem to really exist,' said DC Caffey, tucking her hair behind her ears.

Rebwar leaned back in his chair. 'Go on.'

DC Caffey adjusted her chair. 'Who are you?'

'Was an Uber driver and now work a building site as security.'

DS Hunter pushed the folder to the side and leaned in. 'Now you say this... But what were you doing interviewing Mr Buckham? And DC Smith. Explain.'

'I help her out. I have experience as a policeman.'

DC Caffey flicked through her files. 'When?'

'Iran. You should know all this.'

'How?' said DC Caffey.

Rebwar moved forward and put his elbows on the table. 'What's the charge?'

'Where's your wife?' said DC Caffey. 'And are you having a sexual relationship with Mrs Dinah Sasani?'

'I don't know where my wife is and yes.'

DS Hunter pointed at him with his index finger. 'Your son is called Musa, right? He just called you when we visited. Where is he?'

'He won't tell me. And it would be great if you could find my wife as she was having an affair with Dr Gul.'

They both flicked through their files until DC Caffey found something and whispered into DS Hunter's ear.

'Where were you on the night of the twelfth of November?' said DS Hunter.

'At home.'

'Can anyone testify for you?'

'My flatmates.'

'Did you know Dr Gul?'

'Yes, he was from Iran and my wife's family knew his. She also got a job with him.'

DS Hunter said. 'And we know what happened there.'

'She had left me by then.'

'So you were estranged?'

Rebwar nodded, feeling his anger rise.

'What was your relationship with Dr Gul? Strained? Amicable?'

'Acquaintance. He's helped out in an earlier case.'

DC Caffey looked through her notebook. 'Are you some kind of amateur private detective?'

'No, and I can't comment.'

'Yes, delusions, I would call it. Sure the Home Office is soon going to clear this up,' DS Hunter snapped. He popped his knuckles by stretching them out. DC Caffey grimaced at the sound. 'Now, how did you meet DC Smith?'

'No comment.'

'Look, the more you tell us the sooner you walk out of that door.'

'And into a cell?'

DC Caffey picked up her pen and tapped it on her notepad. 'You do realise that you and your wife are possible suspects.'

Rebwar looked at them and crossed his arms. He'd been wondering when they would say that. But he wasn't going to do their work for them. Although so far he felt he had.

'How did Mike Hays die?' he asked.

'You tell us.'

'Dr Gul, the report said, got hit just here.' And with his hand, Rebwar motioned a strike to the back of the neck. 'And then he fell and broke his neck and he was found in that fatberg.'

Both of them checked their notes.

'So, my theory is that they probably fought. Maybe he didn't have the money or owed them more. And in the struggle, he fell too. It was raining, so slippery and dark.'

'And Buckham?'

'Committed suicide."

'Death by suicide. It's not a sin.'

'Thank you for that, DC Caffey. No note was found and why go to the hassle of drilling a hole in the boot? I mean, just shove it through the window. And in front of his own house?' He shook his head. 'That's a message.'

'See, I think you were involved in this racket,' said DS Hunter. 'Your wife conveniently worked for Dr Gul and you muscled in on it.'

'And why would I kill my dealer?'

'You tell me?'

Rebwar crossed his arms again and leaned back. 'What about Myrian or his ex-partners at KhanWin Beauty?'

'She—'

DS Hunter held out his hand to stop DC Caffey from carrying on. 'What's your relationship with Mrs Gul?'

Rebwar shrugged.

'Did you shag her? Like Mrs Sasani?'

Rebwar looked away. He was trying to get under his skin.

'Bit of a ladies' man? What about in your Uber?'

Rebwar just shook his head. 'Four point seven stars.'

'Right, Mr Ghorbani, is there anything we need to know about your past in Iran?'

'No comment.'

'I bet!'

There was a knock on the door and an officer opened it and called DS Hunter. As he left, DC Caffey announced into the recorder that he had left the room.

'So who do you think did it?' Rebwar said.

'Mr Ghorbani, I am not at liberty to say.' She looked down and wrote something in her notebook.

A few moments later, DS Hunter walked back in and switched off the recording device. 'Powerful friends, Mr Ghorbani – or a damn good lawyer. You are free to go.'

Rebwar got up, adjusted his shirt, and put on his black leather jacket.

As he walked out, DS Hunter said, 'This isn't over. I've got you in my crosshairs.'

Rebwar stared back at them both.

THIRTY-FIVE

Geraldine was at the morgue, sitting in the waiting area. Since calling Highclere for help with Rebwar's run-in with DS Hunter, he had made her go and identify Mike Hays' body. It was something she had been avoiding. She was glad that Highclere had managed to pull some strings to get Rebwar out, but at what cost she didn't yet know. But it was their mess. The place stank of disinfectants and other noxious chemicals. It made her sick. It was sparse, with only a few stiff chairs to sit on and no magazines. She wondered how Beckie was doing. She looked back at her texts and a few made her smile. A text from Sandra flashed up. Guilt covered her like an itchy rash. Her mind swirled around mixing her emotions with rational ideas. She went looking for a snack dispenser which she found down a hallway. Tapped her bank card and put in a number. A bright orange bottle of Lucozade rolled out of the dispenser.

'DC Smith?'

A tall brown-skinned man wearing a turban, with a large dark beard, thick-rimmed glasses, and a white coat walked towards her. She nodded before taking a gulp of the sweet fizzy drink.

'Not a fan? Need a bit more time?'

'No, no, I'll be OK. Been a long week.' Geraldine read his badge. 'Dr Japra.'

'Sorry, where are my manners.' Dr Japra shook her hand. 'Now, you are here to identify Mr Hays. Correct?'

Geraldine nodded.

'You do look a little white. Oh, I mean pale. No offence. Sure you don't need a few more minutes?'

'Let's get on with it.'

They walked off into the morgue. Geraldine sipped her drink, hoping the sugar would kick in like some class A drug. There were three metal slabs and on the middle one was a covered body.

'Now...' Dr Japra held onto the green cover. 'He was found in the Thames and I guess you've seen this before?'

Geraldine nodded again. He pulled back the cover to reveal a half-eaten, white bloated face. She had seen bodies like this before but they always shocked her. She turned away before her stomach would react having also noticed the braided goatee. She nodded and confirmed verbally as she had to. She could feel her mouth salivating. Not a good sign. She took a few more breaths. Beckie would have been laughing her socks off by now.

'Would you rather carry on outside?'

The two were in front of the mortuary, each smoking a cigarette. 'How did he die?'

Dr Japra looked through his iPad. 'There were signs of bruising from a fight and multiple fractures which are common from a fall. He didn't drown but died from multiple internal haemorrhages. He also had opioids in his system as well as alcohol. He might also have been an addict at some point, and by that I mean heroin. Difficult to pin down, but his liver was damaged, and he was HIV positive.'

'Thanks, Doc – I mean Dr Japra. Been interesting.' Geraldine spotted a middle-aged woman walk up to the door with a teenage girl. 'One more question... has Mrs Hays come by?'

Dr Japra tapped on his iPad. 'She's scheduled to come in after you.'

Geraldine looked into the reception area and saw that the wife had gone into the mortuary while the teenage girl was outside sitting opposite on a phone. Geraldine stayed outside having another few cigarettes while waiting for them. It wasn't too long before they were out and Geraldine approached.

'Excuse me, sorry to disturb you.' Geraldine brought out her warrant card and showed it to them. 'Can I ask a few questions?'

The middle-aged blonde woman looked shocked. 'What is it about?'

'About your husband, Mike Hays.'

'You're despicable, you lot. Dragging me out here to see that filth. I'd hoped never to see him again.'

'So you were estranged?'

'Mummy, can we go?'

Geraldine offered a cigarette.

'I've given up.'

Geraldine noticed the daughter eyeing them up but she refrained from offering one. She lit up herself.

'Oh, fuck it! Give me one.' And Mrs Hays took one. 'I blame him. That fucker.'

'Did you know he was involved in opioids?'

'Not really. Turned a blind eye. He's been an addict all

his life. Take one, hun. I know you smoke and it'll shut you up.'

Geraldine offered a cigarette. 'How old is she?'

'Seventeen. Look, I hope you catch those fuckers. Scum. I should have known.'

Geraldine asked the teenage girl. 'Did you know?' She shrugged her shoulders and looked down.

'Oh, don't involve her. She's in enough trouble as it is.'

'Who worked with him?'

'Fucked I know. Some guys. I stayed away, you know what I mean.'

'Steve Buckham?'

'Steve... that's one of them I think. And some other bloke – creepy looking. Always stared at my tits. Got them done in Turkey. Got a nice doctor if you want some.' She winked at Geraldine.

'Jim Jacobi?'

'Jim. That's the creep. Yep, sure he's a paedo. Made sure she was far away when he was about.'

'So what went on?'

'Oh, they would come round and sort out some boxes, have a few beers and watch some shit on the box.'

'Pills?'

'Yeah, from Steve's company, Proxy or something like that. He said it was like those designer stores. Old out-of-fashion stock. Do love a good sale. Got these.' She looked down and showed off her high sparkly heels. 'Some posh designer. Hey, Carol, can you see the label?'

'Jane Achoo or something. Mum, can we go? I've got to meet up—'

'Shush, my sweetheart, this is important police business.' She pulled out a pack of gum and some perfume. 'Gum?'

Geraldine shook her head. 'Mrs—'

'Call me Stacey,' She sprayed perfume all over herself.

Geraldine drew hard on a cigarette and exhaled to shield herself from the incoming sickly smell.

'Where were you on the fourteenth of November?'

'What day was that?'

'Wednesday.'

'With my ladies at the bingo. Every Wednesday rain or shine.'

'And your husband?'

'Fuck knows. Probably out. Didn't see him that week. Didn't see him most weeks and now he's dead.'

Carol Hays' head dropped and her brown hair hid her face. She sniffed.

'Oh, grow up, babes. He was a shit father and you didn't have to see his body.' Mrs Hays looked away and stuck her tongue out like she was puking. 'Got another?'

Geraldine passed her another cigarette.

'You didn't think to report it in?'

'Last time... well see?' And she pointed at her cheekbone. 'Fucking broke it and had to go to Turkey. Got some little extra but no, not again.'

'How do they know each other?'

'You know that puzzled me too. Because their dicks really weren't a match, if you know what I mean. For a while, Mike was a mechanic and I think they met through the garage and pub.'

'Do you think Steve or Jim killed Mike?'

Mrs Hays dragged her cigarette a few times and thought about it. 'Na, Steve's a baby-faced lazy slug and... You know, Jim could have it in him. Mike was the one with the temper. When I heard he'd died I thought it was in some pub fight, glassed by some bouncer or something.'

'Thank you, Mrs Hays and Carol. If you think of anything else, please call me.' Geraldine handed her card over.

'Yeah, thanks, but I'll hide this. Anytime.'

The two walked away to their car, Mrs Hays struggling in her designer shoes.

THIRTY-SIX

Rebwar had got Raj to reach out to Jolly Sweeney's social media account to try to get into contact with some of her friends and it had worked. There was a party happening at the Barrio in Shoreditch in the trendy part of the East End of London. They had said the event was being held in her honour. He had found out about Ms Sweeney from Dr Gul's client list. He'd done some cosmetic work on her as well as probably being her drug dealer. Rebwar had also pulled a favour from his flatmate Genny; as he had a car, he'd agreed to drive them there if they could get him into the party. He also thought that he needed some friends there to look credible instead of like a father looking for his son or daughter. He expected to bring up the average age significantly.

Barrio was on Shoreditch High Street and the area was crowded with young and beautiful people. For him, it was a little like stepping back in time as the eighties fashion was all the rage. Back in Iran, he had only seen it in imported French magazines like OK, Hello, or Elle. Hourieh used to get them sent by her friends around the world. Each bar blared out another catchy beat. Outside under the bright mint green awnings of the Barrio was a line of kids – or that's how Rebwar saw them. Each wore some loud and tight fluorescent garment. The three walked up to the bouncer. Apart from Genny, they had missed the dress code.

'Sorry, it's a private party – invite only,' said the bouncer, a tall, broad black man in sunglasses, even though it was past ten pm.

Rebwar stepped up to him. 'We are invited, Rebwar, Raj and Genny. Friends of Jolly.'

The man lowered his glasses and looked over the top of them. 'Wait here.' He turned around and whistled over to a girl. She was slim with slick black hair and wore a black tuxedo with apparently nothing under it.

'Roxy!' said Raj. 'Rocking the place.' And he finger slapped.

'Raj? Dude, you guys made it. So dope you could make it yah, yah.' She waved them to come in.

The bouncer stopped Rebwar and frisked him. Once he was happy, he motioned him in.

Inside, the place was an explosion of colours and angular shapes. Mint green, reds, yellows, blues – it all screamed out, which added to the vibe. There was a long bar with a line of different cocktails waiting to be picked. Genny took two and so did Raj. Roxy kept walking and Rebwar followed her through the crowd. Raj and Genny didn't know where to look; the place was filled with models, all dressed immaculately. At the back was an outside area that was Astroturf and had multicoloured benches, exotic-looking potted plants and painted murals.

'Guys, guys,' Roxy got the attention of a little crowd sitting on one of the benches. They were all barely twenty and wore tight-fitting shirts and trousers with sweatbands or armbands. Even one of the girls had leg warmers. 'This is Raj and…'

Raj carried on with the introduction. 'My Uncle Rebwar and Genny from Brazil.'

All of them in unison said, 'Hi, Uncle and Genny.'

One of the guys stood up and went over to Rebwar and put his arm around his neck. 'So, Uncle, heard you were tight with old Dr Gul.'

'He was from my country.'

'Dope, man, that's dope! Has he gone back?' He tapped his nose and winked.

'No, he was… passed away. An accident.'

'Fuck, you being real? No, that's sick shit. Sorry to hear, bro.'

'You knew him?'

He motioned his head in a circular motion. 'You know, Jolly did.' And he picked up a shot glass and raised it to his little crowd. 'Jolly, Jolly, Jolly, Jolly, Ho!' and they all downed a shot. Others behind them joined in and a second round of shots were knocked back.

The guy sniffed and closed in again. 'Right, so you got some?'

Raj came over to Rebwar and discreetly put a little bag of pills into his hand. Rebwar put it into his pocket. He now understood under what promise Raj had gotten them in. And the bouncer had taken the bait. 'I've got a little present, no charge, in memory of Jolly. But who else knew the doctor? You know I need to introduce myself.' Rebwar slipped the bag into his hand.

'Comprende, my friend, I'll make some introductions for you.'

Rebwar was left chatting to a girl who was barely older

than his son. She kept asking about what gear he had. Rebwar politely introduced Genny and went to find Roxy who was a few tables down.

'Did you know Dr Gul?' said Rebwar.

'You're Raj's uncle?'

'And?'

'You give me the creeps.'

'So what happened to Jolly?'

Roxy stepped back and looked at him.

'I'm here to help.'

'She was my girlfriend.'

'I'm investigating her death.'

Roxy stared at him. 'Did Dr Gul kill her?' She grabbed a drink that passed by on a tray, to the annoyance of the waitress.

'Tell me.'

'She...' Roxy gulped her drink down. 'She was damaged after seeing Dr Gul. Addicted. Not the same. I... I couldn't handle her.'

'Drugs?'

Roxy stepped back.

'I'm not a drug dealer...'

She sipped her drink and looked around her. 'Raj said...'

'Roxy, listen to me... there's a killer out there and I'm going to find him, OK?'

The music ramped up 'What?'

'When was the last time you saw Jolly?'

'What?'

Rebwar realised it was hopeless. The party had ramped up and everyone was losing control. A waiter passed by carrying a tray full of drinks, Rebwar grabbed one and sipped it. It tasted sweet and had an undefined kick to it. He texted Dinah.

Rebwar asked Raj. 'Got any leads?'

'Uncle, they all loves Dr Gul. He was a legend.'

Rebwar looked over to the end of the patio and saw Dinah. She was wearing one of the white flowing dresses from her boutique. For a moment, the music stopped and everyone stared.

THIRTY-SEVEN

Geraldine sat in the KhanWin waiting room looking at the glossy brochures on what enhancing procedures they offered. She smiled remembering that Sandra had had surgery. She'd had them done because of a cancer scare she'd had a few years before. Geraldine had stepped into that one as she had made fun of them and thought it was on a man's whim. Dr Edwin Norwin walked up to her and asked her to come into his office. He was short with salt and pepper hair, which was immaculately styled with a side parting. His smiling head looked huge on his slight frame. He wore a navy pinstripe three-piece suit.

'What can I do for you?'

'This is a police matter.' She put her warrant card on his desk.

His smile dropped and he looked at her ID. 'Did, did we schedule this?' He tapped away at his computer.

'No, I dropped in. I'm investigating the murder of Dr Gul.'

Norwin leaned forward and interlocked his hands. 'I've answered your questions with your colleague and will only answer more questions with my solicitor present.'

'Only if you have something to hide and it's just some follow-ups, sorry for the inconvenience.' Geraldine had managed to get a transcript from DS Hunter's files. High-clere had done the decent thing and shared information. And it had surprised her; she guessed Plan B had turned over a new leaf.

'You say that Dr Gul had been using confidential client information to sell illicit drugs. Don't you all share client information within the practice?'

'Look, we don't sell illicit drugs and we had an under-standing that his clients were his and mine, mine.'

'Did you know about Dr Khan' affairs?'

'I don't pry into his private life.'

'But it's interfering with this practice isn't it?' Geraldine stood up and walked towards a bookcase filled with bound medical books.

'I... I'm not sure what you're asking?'

'His affair with Myrian Gul. Odd, no? And a little awkward. Sure you've had a few discussions.' Geraldine checked her notes. 'Ms Boyd said that she had seen you two arguing over it.'

'Yes, well that was... a couple of months ago. And I wasn't comfortable with that. We had just parted with Dr Gul.'

'Was that the real reason why you parted ways?'

Norwin gave a nervous stuttering laugh. 'No, no, he was selling opioids to our clients without our knowledge. We had to act.'

'And you didn't report it to the police?' Geraldine checked out one of the office plants. It was plastic and had a sheen of dust on it.

'Like I said to one of your colleagues, we couldn't because of legal reasons and wanted to keep this quiet. Imagine what it would have done to this practice.'

'Yes, but look where you are now?'

'What do you mean?'

'Do you think Dr Khan has it in him to kill Dr Gul? As a medic, it's easy to overstep the mark, no?'

'We have an oath. No!' Norwin hit his fist on the glass office table.

'Who do you think could have done it?'

'Sorry, but I have no idea. Isn't that your job, DS Smith?'

'My job is to ask questions, Dr Norwin. Are you gay?'

'Frankly, that is none of your business and I don't see how it affects this case.'

'I think Dr Gul knew that and used it against you. I think he was a divisive figure and got you all bickering.'

'I agree that he was a difficult man, but we dealt with it.'

Geraldine saw a couple of small bottles of water and asked if he minded and took one.

'So what was your turnover before with Dr Gul and now?'

'I would have to ask my accountant.'

'Roughly thirty per cent drop or fifty...' Geraldine looked at the plants. 'From what I can see you've cut costs.'

'We're working on that. Yes, it's been a difficult time.'

'Can I guess that you've lost a lot of clients? Checked out your Google reviews—'

'DS Smith, frankly I'm getting tired of you making us look guilty. You should be out there catching the killer.'

'Where were you on the fourteenth of November?' Geraldine checked her notes; he had said at the movies with a friend called Mark.

'I thought I'd answered that.' He clicked the computer's mouse and tapped his keyboard. 'Cinema.'

'What did you see and can anyone corroborate?'

'You should check your files, DS Smith. I sent a bank statement with the transaction and my good friend... Ian was with me.'

'Moonlight?'

'Sorry? Oh, the film... it was... I can't remember.' Norwin looked around his desk as if the answer was there. 'I'll have to ask...'

'Mark?'

Norwin's fist tightened and he squeezed the bridge of his nose. 'Sorry, been a long few weeks.'

'Can I get his number?'

'Who?'

'The man you're seeing.'

'DS...' Norwin let out a sigh.

'Who else knows?'

'No one, really no one.'

Geraldine leaned in. 'Look, I understand. I came out a couple of years ago. It's not the end of the world. And frankly, you'll probably get more business – certainly, new business.'

'You interested?'

Geraldine laughed and shook her head. 'Dr Norwin, what are you implying? I like my middle-age spread. Although...' She looked at her notes again. 'Tell me about Ms Maddox.'

'Attesa? Good hard-working girl. Sweet and—'

'Did Khan settle with Ms Maddox?'

'I couldn't possibly comment. You'll have to ask him and her.'

Geraldine got up. 'Thank you, Dr Norwin, and I hope I

don't have to see you at the station. If there is anything you want to add, please call me.' She put her card on the table. She wasn't going to get any more out of him and had proved a point.

THIRTY-EIGHT

Rebwar was by a crossing on Harley Street smoking a cigarette. To his left was the exit to an underground garage. A blue Porsche pulled out onto the street and he spotted Dr Khan at the wheel. It stopped at the lights and he went up to it and knocked on the window. It lowered and Rebwar reached in to open the door from the inside. He sat down on the passenger seat.

'Hey! Get out of my car...' Dr Khan's expression changed to one of surprise. 'You're that private detective.'

'Drive.'

'What? No! You get out of my car. Now!.'

'Dr Khan, drive and I'll be asking the questions.'

Cars honked behind them.

'No! I'm calling the police.'

'I wouldn't recommend that. You're one of the suspects.'

'Me?'

The honking intensified.

'Drive and I'll talk.'

Dr Khan looked ahead and drove off. The car smelled

new and felt expensive with its black leather and chrome details.

'What's your relationship with Ms Maddox?'

'She's a colleague.'

'What's the monthly payment.'

'Her salary? She's an employee.'

'And an extra ten thousand going to an offshore account under the name of Apollo Fund and she's a shareholder.'

'It's an investment. Why? Am I a suspect Mr…?'

'Eyes front, and it's Rebwar. You forced yourself on her, didn't you?'

'I'm calling my lawyer. This is not happening.'

'Myrian's told me everything. I knew them both. Did you kill Dr Gul?'

Dr Khan tried to use his phone, but the traffic and stress were making him miss the screen.

'Listen, I don't think you did, but you are involved somehow. Was he blackmailing you?'

'Khan stopped the car just off a bus stop. 'Get out, now!' He tried to grab Rebwar's arm. He lunged across and pulled the door lever, which opened the door. Rebwar grabbed his neck and squeezed hard.

'You're hurting me. Get off me.'

Rebwar closed the door and kept applying pressure to Khan's neck, squeezing his left main artery.

'Let go, let go!'

Rebwar felt him losing his energy and he let go.

'Fuck sake, are you some kind of orangutan?'

'What happened with Ms Maddox?'

'We dated, and then she tried to sue me.'

'She let us into the practice and after that payments started appearing in an offshore account. There's only a couple of reasons that would happen. As she told me. Who else?'

Dr Khan rubbed his neck and breathed in deeply. 'Yes, I'm an idiot, but I've dealt with it.'

'Did Dr Gul know?'

Dr Khan nodded.

'Does Myrian know?'

'You said...' He slumped his head down. 'Yes.'

'And you used her to get to him.'

'No, no, I love her. Are they going to arrest me?'

'Probably. What happened on the fourteenth?'

'I lost him... Yes, we followed him. Myrian and I.'

'Where?'

'I don't know—'

'Where? Think!' Rebwar lowered the passenger window and lit a cigarette.

'Hey! Not in here.'

'Then tell me. Did you wait for him at his home?'

'Yes. And he didn't come back. But we couldn't really call it in. We checked the next day and he still wasn't there. We thought he'd done a runner.'

'What were you going to do to him?'

'Nothing, just... just scare him a little. You know, he was a shit and wanted more money. From both of us.'

'And Hourieh? Was she there in the car you followed?'

'That bitch?' And his face changed. 'Oh, sorry... I for—'

Rebwar felt a flush of anger, which didn't make sense to him as, frankly, she had been. 'How?'

'She... She schemed with him. She was involved.'

'Was she at his home on that night?'

'They went together—'

'And my son, Musa?'

Dr Khan held the steering wheel. 'I think he was left in the house.'

Rebwar's fists clenched.

'I didn't know... I thought it was their child. I would have called social services if I'd known.'

'What about Myrian?'

'She wanted to expose Amin.'

Rebwar also knew that she had met Musa and, as she had lost her child with Dr Gul, she must have been very angry to see that.

'Have you got kids?'

'No.'

'And what about Dr Norwin?'

'Yes, two.'

Rebwar lit another cigarette like he had done in his mate's cars back in Iran. Especially if they still had that new car smell about them. He got a childish thrill out of it, and it wound Khan up.

'Hey!'

'And you never saw Hourieh or Musa again?'

'No.'

At least Rebwar knew they were all right, but now he understood why she was hiding.

'Who else was involved?

'No one.'

'Norwin? Ms Maddox? Ms Boyd?'

'They were there when we let Dr Gul go and through the arguments.'

'Drive. Otherwise, the police are going to become suspicious. They have cameras.'

Dr Khan put the car into drive and pulled out into the traffic. The car's wipers flicked across the windscreen. Rebwar looked around him.

'Take a left here and then a right.'

They were down a quiet little one-way side street. He looked behind. Only a few pedestrians and closed shutters.

'Keep going and take a left at the end.'

'Who's after you?'

'They are after you, my friend.' It was a lie, although he was still surprised that DS Hunter hadn't taken him.

'What... what should I do?'

'Go in and tell them.'

'But I'm innocent.' Khan re-joined a busy road.

'Take another left here.' Rebwar looked behind and saw a van follow them. 'Right here and then left.'

'I was just trying to scare him off. He ruined us, you understand, we have debts.'

'Stop the car here.'

Khan pulled up behind another car. The van passed them. Rebwar noted the number plate and watched it drive on.

'You could have taken him to court.'

'No. It would have been too embarrassing.'

'Why?'

'He could have exposed all the lawsuits and...'

'And you. Ms Maddox and others... And Ms Boyd, was she—'

'No, that was Dr Gul. They had something... Colluding, gossiping.'

'Why is she still there?'

Dr Khan pointed to the glove box. Rebwar opened it and saw that there was a silver hip flask. He passed it over, and Khan took a large gulp out of it. Offered it to Rebwar.

'I think you need it.'

'Ms Boyd fell out with Dr Gul... something happened.

But she's got a stake in the practice and we didn't have the money to pay her off.'

'Do you know who killed Dr Gul?'

'No idea, I... we got scared.'

'Watch your back, there is a killer out there. You need to talk to the police.'

Dr Khan took a couple of large gulps from his flask. Rebwar watched him take deep breaths.

'You OK?'

'No, no.'

'Call your lawyer.' Rebwar stepped out of the car and walked off.

THIRTY-NINE

Rebwar was back in his home, sitting at the kitchen table sipping a bottle of Becks beer. Which he had just bought at the little supermarket down the road. He was thinking back over the case and felt he'd missed something obvious. But just couldn't put his finger on it. Jesus came in smoking a joint and went up to the fridge.

'Mind if I take a beer?'

'Sure.' Rebwar smelled the sweet smoke. Which made him think of the newsagents that he'd visited on King's Road, where Dr Gul had sold some of his opioids. It gave him an idea to go back there. 'Jesus, mind if I borrow your mobile for a call?'

'Out of credits?'

'Want someone to pick up.'

'Yeah, sure. Whatever.' Jesus put his phone on the table and opened his beer.

Rebwar dialled Hourieh's number. He lit his cigarette, felt his hands go cold, and a wave of nausea fill him. He'd been hiding behind Musa. The phone rang. Jesus watched him. He let it ring till a standard voicemail message came on. He dropped the call and passed over the phone with a mix of relief and disappointment.

'Girlfriend?' asked Jesus.

'Wife...' Rebwar lit another cigarette and stared at Jesus. 'How do you know?'

'About the girlfriend?'

Rebwar nodded and guessed. 'Genny told you?'

'She's a hot milf, man.'

Of course, Genny had shown him pictures, and he just hoped he hadn't posted anything on Facebook. He should have mentioned it. Jesus's phone rang, and he showed him the number.

Rebwar took it. 'Hello.'

'Husband?'

'Yes. You were with Amin the night he was murdered.'

There was a long moment of silence till she answered. 'Yes... but—'

'Were you there?'

'Not really, no. Just in the car.'

'Why didn't you tell me... all this time, and I had to find out like this!'

Rebwar heard her sigh and then light a cigarette. 'I was embarrassed... ashamed... Husband, I couldn't. I was unhappy—'

'We could have talked about it. And Musa?'

Jesus got another beer from the fridge and left the kitchen. Rebwar held his forehead. 'Wife... I don't recognise you anymore. What were you thinking?'

'I want attention. Love. Feel like a wife that is there... not a piece of furniture. Like some stove that you use to get your belly full. You understand?'

Rebwar tapped his cigarette into the empty beer can. 'What did you do when you found out about Amin?'

'What's the point? He was taken away from me.'

Rebwar swore to himself. 'You are in danger, understand? And Musa. I don't know who killed him.'

'It was an accident…'

'How do you know this?'

'I went to see, and there was Amin and another man at the bottom of the hole. And I left them.'

'Didn't you think to call me?'

'And say what?'

'Woman, I was going to find out.'

'And now you're having an affair with Dinah – my best friend! How dare you tell me what to do.'

Rebwar now knew the answer to the gossip.

'You are going to apologise to Musa.'

'Hourieh, don't drag our son into our dirty laundry.' But it was too late she was calling out his name. Rebwar hesitated on dropping the call, but he had to speak to his son.

'Father, how's it going?'

'Musa, good to hear your voice. Been good at school?'

'Yeah, new friends, but it's OK.'

'Moved again?'

Musa was silent.

'It's all right I'm not going to ask you where you are. Your mother…' Rebwar held back. 'I have to tell you something.'

'Yes, Dad.'

'I'm seeing Dinah.'

'Dad… OK. I… Why?'

'I'm lonely. I miss you guys and…' Rebwar took another deep breath. 'Can you pass your mother?'

'Husband, you made your bed now you can… you know what.'

'You know the police are going to talk to you. They know.'

'That doesn't surprise me. You told them, didn't you? Rat.'

'No, and I'm still protecting you.'

'Rebwar, you do what you need to do.' She dropped the call.

He stared at the screen and closed his eyes.

'Falling asleep?'

Rebwar looked up to see Genny.

'No, just had to tell my son about Dinah.'

'Oh, shit, bro... I... thought it was. You know.'

'It's done.'

'Great party, though. What a crowd. And you hang out with those dudes... They like to party.' He laughed. 'And I'm saying party.'

'You stay for the after-party?'

'Yeah,' Genny's eyes lit up. 'Fuck, dope that was. Tunes and drugs.'

'Like?'

'Pills and lines. They are animals.'

'I saw you talk to that black girl... Brazilian?'

'Well spotted, my friend. From the north, exotic. Alanza.' And he got out his phone and showed him some pictures he had posted on Facebook. She had thick black curly hair that covered half her pretty face.

'You spoke to her for a while. Friendly?'

Genny pointed his index finger at him. 'How do you say... plays for other team.' And he winked at him.

'Say anything about Jolly?'

Genny went to the fridge and took one of Rebwar's beers and pulled up a chair to sit down.

'You're welcome...' Rebwar stared at the Becks can he had just opened.

'Sorry?'

Rebwar liked to sometimes tease Genny with the British ways to which he was oblivious. 'Cheers.' He raised his beer.

'You know she got hooked on opioids?'

'Alanza?'

'No, she's clean. Jolly. Sad story, man.'

'Go on.'

'She had a couple of plastic jobs.' Genny held his hands like he was holding a set of large breasts. 'And nose, but this Dr Gul; one of them got infected. Bad, hospital. And he gave her these pills to make the pain go away.'

'Opioids?'

'Like heroin, crazy stuff and it's legit. Bad story. She was hooked like a junkie.'

Rebwar didn't know what to say. He should never have given them to that boy even if it was for information. He felt he had overstepped the line.

'Did you take some?'

'Na, man, since hearing Alanza... and she was angry. Jolly was giving them out to her friends because she wanted to get high with them. Dr Death that's what he should be called. Fucked up. Man, man, sad story.'

Rebwar drank his beer, wanting to forget. It hadn't been a good day and he was emotionally drained. He got up and told Genny he was going to his bed. But he knew that he was going to be lucky if he managed an hour or two of sleep.

FORTY

Rebwar returned to the newsagents on King's Road as he wanted to find out more about Dr Gul's operation. Something had happened on that night when Mike Hays delivered the boxes of opioids. He walked into the old stuffy store, stocked up with international magazines and newspapers, and some cold cabinets with basic necessities like milk, fizzy drinks and beer. Rebwar greeted the young man behind the counter. He replied in English and had dark rings around his eyes and looked scruffy.

'Like to see the boss.'

'Who's asking?'

'Say it's...' Rebwar headed to the back for the side door.

'Hey!'

Rebwar went down the small spiral staircase and a strong smell of cannabis smoke hit him. He saw that Hussein was stacking some boxes.

'Rebwar, what took you so long?'

'I was waiting for you to call.'

Hussein grabbed a rolled-up joint from the ashtray on a small metal table. 'Find your man?'

'No, who delivers?'

'Listen, I have been here since 1964. You have no right and ask me questions like a corrupt policeman. I have dealt with you people, many years and you all the same. I am still here.'

Rebwar lit up and looked around the small dark, damp cellar. 'Low on Poroxy?'

He shrugged.

'I can get you some more.'

Hussein sat down and tapped his cigarette in the glass ashtray. 'Tell me more.' He lit two scented tea lights.

'How many boxes do you need?'

Hussein looked over at a pile of various sized boxes and counted with his fingers and showed him seven. He lit his joint and dragged on it.

Rebwar knew that there were a couple at Bijan's and Dr Gul's houses. He was interested to see where this would go. He could see that Hussein had three left and, from Buckham's records, they lost between sixty to seventy boxes a year, which was probably an underestimation. Rebwar thought closer to a hundred.

'When was the last delivery?'

Hussein looked up. 'Three months ago.'

Which meant he was worried and wanted to stock up. If he got three every couple of months, Rebwar reckoned that he would have at least eighteen a year. Which meant he was one of about eight clients that Dr Gul had. Rebwar held up three fingers.

Hussein rubbed his greying moustache. 'When can you deliver?'

'Tomorrow.'

'On delivery, two thousand.' Hussein put his hand out, waiting for Rebwar to shake it.

'I'm not a charity.'

'OK, I understand. Difficult times. Three.'

'I have other clients.'

'For a friend from the homeland.'

Rebwar stood up. 'I'm offering below asking price. Also, who was the Persian woman with Amin?'

'Pretty woman. Have seen her before. Buys dope from me.'

Rebwar showed him a picture of Dinah.

'Yes, yes that's her.' And he smiled and winked at him.

'When?'

'A few months ago.'

'Did she make the introduction?'

'Why...' Hussein looked at him for a moment. 'She got better price.'

Rebwar stared at him.

'You killed him. It makes sense now.' Hussein got up and stepped back to a glass counter behind him, where shish and other marijuana accessories were displayed. 'You came to trick me. Stupid of me. I should have listened. It was you. Yes, it all makes sense.'

Rebwar looked behind him to see Dr Norwin standing by the stairs.

'We are closed...' Hussein made his way behind the cabinet.

'Listen, Hussein, you're not thinking straight.' Rebwar turned to Norwin. 'And what are you doing here?'

Hussein brought out a cricket bat and held it up. Norwin took out his phone.

'I can help. I don't think either of you killed Dr Gul.' Which he wasn't sure was true but he had to reassure them.

'It was you. You want to sell me his stock and you are

jealous because he took your wife. It makes sense, don't you think mister?'

'Dr Norwin.'

'He worked with Amin.'

Rebwar noticed Hussein's bloodshot eyes and dilated pupils. He was high and feeling anxious. He'd seen it all too often.

'You too?'

'No, I'm looking for his...'

'What are you looking for?' said Rebwar.

'I think I've found what I needed.' And Dr Norwin made his way up the stairs.

Rebwar ran over and grabbed his hoodie before he could get further up and tugged him back down to the floor. And felt a hard thud on his right shoulder blade. He turned around to see that Hussein had hit him with his cricket bat. Rebwar grabbed a cardboard box and blocked his next swing. Dr Norwin got up and grabbed the box off Rebwar who kicked Hussein's leg. Off balance, his bat missed and hit the stone floor. Rebwar punched Dr Norwin in the chest and with his elbow hit Hussein square in his jaw. He stumbled back, knocking the table and falling onto the glass cabinet. Norwin, doubled down on the floor, was trying to grab his phone which Rebwar stamped on with his heel.

Rebwar noticed smoke around him. Hussein was trying to prop himself off the glass cabinet that leaned on the back wall. Dr Norwin was holding his chest. Flames appeared around some of the stacked cardboard boxes. The tea lights had fallen off the table. Rebwar looked around for a fire extinguisher. He ran up the spiral staircase into the shop.

'Fire. Where is—'

'No, no, we... no.' The young man at the till stepped back, seeing smoke rise from the stairs.

'Call the fire brigade.'

The young man ran out of the shop.

Rebwar went back down the stairs and saw a hand come through the thickening smoke. He grabbed it. Norwin grabbed his other hand and he pulled him up the stairs. He was coughing and still struggling to breathe. With his jacket sleeve over his mouth, Rebwar went back down the stairs but the smoke was too thick to see. He shouted Hussein's name. All he could hear was a raging fire taking hold of the boxes. He headed reluctantly back upstairs and called 999.

FORTY-ONE

Geraldine looked down at her phone and tried to work out where she was. Highclere had told her to meet on Parliament Hill. She'd never been there and all she could see were trees, a couple of tarmacked paths, a green open space, squirrels and people walking their dogs. It was also hilly, and she was out of breath and frustrated. What was wrong with a coffee place or pub? She chose one of the paths and followed it. She knew it would have probably been easier to ask someone as there weren't any signs or location markers. But she'd watched other people question dog walkers, and it ended up with them looking around and pointing in a direction. It felt a humiliation too far. She watched two men holding hands walk past. It made her think of Beckie and so she called her. It went to voicemail.

'Hey, babes... I'm sorry I haven't called. It's been busy... you know... I guess you don't. Be great to hear from you. Love...' She choked. 'You.'

Her breathing became heavier as the path steepened. A jogger passed her and she stopped to take a few breaths. She couldn't remember the last time she'd been out for a walk that involved inclines. She carried on till she got to the summit. The view was spectacular. People were taking selfies of each other and admiring the view over London. She stopped to look and see her favourite skyscrapers. It was all there from Canary Wharf to the City.

'Impressive, don't you think?'

Geraldine turned around to see Highclere holding a bottle of mineral water and wearing a hoodie, shorts, white socks, trainers, and aviator sunglasses.

'Highclere... Yes. You ran here?'

'It's part of my routine. Shall we walk and talk?' And he led the way down the hill. 'I asked to meet you because I'd like to know what happened at that newsagents.'

'There was a scuffle and a candle caught some cardboard boxes.'

Highclere stopped and faced her. 'Look, I'm not just going to take any old story. I'm getting some heat on this.'

'What are you expecting? A typed report?'

'Will do, but first I want to hear it. Go on.' And he carried on walking.

Geraldine watched two mothers, each pushing a pram, stare at Highclere. 'Rebwar... sorry, I mean The Robin, went to see Hussein, the owner. He wanted to know more about Dr Gul's operation. We found out that they were—'

'They?'

'Buckham and his gang.'

Highclere nodded.

'But we don't think they are linked. Dr Gul was their client.'

'And you think Hussein was trying to go direct.'

'No. But we got a handle on how much he was delivering. Hussein was the local dealer for the Arab and Persian community. Been in business since the seventies.'

Highclere lowered his sunglasses and looked over them. 'Fuck. So who's been protecting him?'

Geraldine shrugged.

'Well, find out. This is going to bite us in the arse. Remember, low key.' He rubbed his jaw. 'Go on.'

'The Robin was interrogating him and Dr Norwin came around unannounced. We think doing his own investigating. This caused a standoff and Hussein had been smoking dope and had been for years and got some kind of anxiety attack, which caused a scuffle and a candle was knocked and it all went up in smoke. And Hussein died in the fire.'

'Right, right, an accident. But it's going to be seen as a gangland attack. And the killer in all this?'

'We have suspects, but no concrete evidence. And what's the deal with DS Hunter's parallel investigation? Some kind of new trial? Isn't this a waste of resources?'

'Look, keep in your lane. It doesn't concern you.'

Geraldine bit her tongue and let it go but it frustrated her. It made no sense to her.

'Are we ready to arrest?' Highclere drank some of his mineral water.

'Not yet. Is DS Hunter?'

'I think so, but I can't say yet.'

'Shouldn't we arrest first? I mean, you know lawyers.'

'We have to tread carefully. I can't keep having to cover your arses. I'm already having to wipe The Robin's prints off the databases.'

Geraldine felt her phone vibrate and saw that it was Beckie calling. She let it ring. 'What do you propose we do?'

'Propose? Your job. Bring in the killer. I thought The Robin had the perfect credentials for this job.'

'We're close, a few more days. Who's he arresting?'

Highclere went up to a tree and with his prosthetic arm leant on it and stretched out his calves. 'Mrs Ghorbani.'

'Fuck! And you tell me now? No, no, we need to talk to her first.'

'Well, I suggest you find her ASAP.' Highclere looked at his watch, pressed some buttons on it and jogged off.

Geraldine watched him and took out her phone. Beckie rang again and she picked up. 'Babes, how are you?'

'I've checked myself out.'

'Why?'

'I need a new perspective. Realised that I was in a toxic life.'

Geraldine looked around as if Beckie was there somewhere. 'Can we meet?'

'No, I'm not in London. Sorry.'

Geraldine tried to hear any background noises that would give her a clue as to her whereabouts. 'You always wanted to go to the sea. Remember? Margate and us running into that cafe?'

'Look, I can't tell you where I've gone. I have to move on. Understand?'

'No, Beckie, I don't. I thought we could give it another go. I'm here for you. Babes, what did they say?'

'I'm sorry. I need time. Time away from all the madness. I feel better and—'

Geraldine heard some voices in the background trying to get Beckie's attention. 'I need to go. Love you.'

'Lo–' The line cut off. Geraldine slumped down on a bench and leaned back.

Her phone rang again. It was Rebwar.

FORTY-TWO

Rebwar was leant against a garden railing smoking a cigarette in Markham Square opposite Myrian Gul's house and on a call.

'I've seen Dr Khan just walk into Myrian's house.'

'Just met Highclere.'

'How did that go?'

'We need to find Hourieh, DS Hunter is going to arrest her.'

'That idiot. Didn't you tell him not to?'

'He doesn't like hearing problems. I'll do some digging see if I can find some clues.'

'Thanks. We could have given them Khan or Norwin to make them waste some time. Maybe try that.'

Geraldine agreed and hung up. Rebwar stubbed out his cigarette on the metal railing and flicked it into the gutter. He crossed the road and rang Myrian's doorbell. He heard some light footsteps and she opened the door.

'Fancy seeing you here. What can I do for you?'

'I need to talk to you and Dr Khan.'

'He's not here—'

'I just saw him come in.'

'Look, I know you're trying to help but I don't need any.'

Rebwar stepped closer and blocked the door with his foot. 'He's told me and you're in this mess. Now let's talk about this and see who's not guilty.'

'I'm not comfortable with this.'

Rebwar shouted Dr Khan's name, telling him to come to see him.

'This is a police matter,' Myrian said, 'and not something for a wannabe detective. And I know why—'

'Let him in,' said Khan, standing in silhouette at the end of the hallway.

Myrian looked back and reluctantly opened the door a little further. Rebwar walked in.

All three stood in the living room, Khan with his arms crossed and Myrian with one hand on her hip. It was like a standoff between them.

'Shall we sit?' said Rebwar.

'Let's see what you've got to say.'

'Sorry would be a start – and to Dinah,' said Myrian.

'What's up with Dinah?'

'You well know.'

Rebwar tried to get an answer from her. He hadn't spoken to her for a day or two. 'Let's stick to the facts.'

'So, who killed my husband?'

'Myrian, why were you following him and Hourieh?'

'We—'

Rebwar held up his hand to Dr Khan. 'I'm asking the question to Myrian.'

She looked over to Dr Khan. 'We wanted to teach him a lesson.'

'And?'

'We were going to get the practice's property back. He'd stolen from all of us.'

'Property?'

'She means—'

'One more word and...' Rebwar showed him some cable ties. 'Go on.'

'Sorry, Vivek,' Myrian looked down. 'We thought we could sell the pills. I mean, he'd stolen, and we needed the money.'

'No, no,' said Khan. 'We were going to take them back for a reward. We weren't going to sell them like common criminals.'

'Myrian, when you found them, what happened?'

'We spotted Hourieh in Amin's car. So we went up to it and confronted her. She reacted badly. It became a heated argument and—'

'I'm calling my lawyer now, Myrian. Don't say any more.'

Rebwar grabbed Dr Khan's phone off him and pushed him against the wall. He didn't resist.

'Rebwar, think about what you're doing. I am going to sue. You won't see Musa again. Understand?'

Rebwar cable-tied Khan's hands behind his back and made him sit reclining in a chair. He looked uncomfortable and tried to wriggle out of his bind.

'Rebwar, please can't we just...' Myrian was torn between helping Dr Khan and talking. 'I didn't want anyone to get hurt. But she just wouldn't shut up.'

'What are you saying?'

'He had to hit her to shut her up. She was shouting over to Amin like a crazy woman. And... and he knocked her out and she looked dead. She was bleeding.'

Rebwar looked over to Dr Khan for a reaction.

'We panicked and put her in the car. It was raining.' Myrian looked at her hands. 'Yes, and we just panicked and left.'

'Myrian, please call the lawyer. We don't have to do this.'

She sat down on a sofa and looked out onto the green garden. 'I want to, I can't carry this secret. We have to tell the truth.'

'And you didn't see anyone else?'

Myrian shook her head.

'When did you realise they were missing?'

'We didn't but... Oh God, I'm sorry.' Tears streamed down Myrian's face. 'I'm so ashamed, she could have died and... Musa, your poor child. Sorry.'

'And you, Khan? Is that what happened or did you go and confront Amin? Is that what happened? An accident?'

Myrian sobbed and Khan tried to get up, but Rebwar pushed him back.

'You could have called it in. You're a doctor, don't you have an oath?'

'I heard it was you. It's you who should be working on your alibi.'

Rebwar grabbed his arm and made him stand up. 'We never got to the reason why you were in that newsagents. Crept in like a little cockroach. You know what I think? You were there trying to get some of Amin's Peroxy boxes. How did you find the address?'

'I want to see my lawyer. Not answering any more of your baseless accusations. Take me to the police and we can sort it out. Go on, hit me then. Go on, I know you want to. Beat a confession out of me. It'll be worthless, you know.'

'You knocked out my wife and left her for dead,

knowing my son was alone in Amin's house. You've got a nerve.'

Rebwar looked over to Myrian. She was on the phone, facing away from them. He let go of Khan, went over to her and grabbed the phone.

'Who is this?'

'Sorry?'

'You heard. Who are you?'

'Simon Hearford, of FDH solicitors. Can you pass my client?'

Rebwar ended the call. 'Myrian, do you know where Hourieh is? Or anyone that might?'

Myrian shook her head.

Rebwar walked over to the living room door and before stepping out said, 'Does Norwin know what you were up to or anyone else in the practice?'

Khan said, 'I told Norwin. It was his idea to try to find the Poroxy.'

Rebwar made his way out.

FORTY-THREE

Rebwar went down the stairs to the Bijan's kitchen. He'd pretended to be delivering a parcel and been let in by a member of the staff. As he got there, a thin young man opened the door. He wore a white double-breasted short-sleeved shirt and a blue and white apron.

'Delivery?'

'I'm looking for Manish?'

'And you are?'

'Rebwar. Old friend of the boss.' Rebwar put his head around the door and called out for Manish.

'Mate, hold on.' The thin man looked at him cautiously. 'I'll get him. Can you wait here?' He pointed at the doormat.

'Sure, sure.' Rebwar held his hands up and got himself a pack of cigarettes.

Manish came to the threshold. 'Rebwar?'

He offered Manish a cigarette and he took one.

'I came by a week or so ago. About those boxes. The ones you are keeping for Dr Gul.'

Manish smiled and nodded. 'Yes, yes. How is he?'

'Dead.'

'You say dead?'

Rebwar nodded. 'Still have those boxes?'

'No. A friend came to pick up. He said he worked with him.'

'Get his name?'

'He was a white man, English.'

Rebwar flicked through his phone and brought up a picture of Buckham.

Manish shook his head. 'Doctor, he said.'

Rebwar showed him a picture of Dr Khan and he shook his head again. Rebwar flicked the screen. 'Him?' He pointed to the screen.

'Yes, that the man.'

It was Dr Norwin. 'When did he pick up the boxes?'

'Yesterday, in a rush.'

Rebwar texted Geraldine to tell her that Dr Norwin had stolen some of Dr Gul's Poroxy boxes. And he went upstairs to go and surprise his old Bijan.

———

He was made to wait in the large living room overlooking the garden. Bijan's butler had not been pleased with him sneaking into the house. Rebwar looked at some pictures of Bijan when he was in the military in Iran. It brought bad memories of the war, something he had struggled with all his life. Weirdly, it had been talking about the conflict with Bijan that had helped him the most. He struggled to remember but slowly had come to terms with it. Like a wound with a scab; at some point, it would fall off without it bleeding – he was still waiting.

'Soldier, my friend! Good to see you. I have been

waiting for your visit.' Walking stick in hand, Bijan walked over to the drinks cabinet.

'Sorry for not announcing myself. I'm busy with Amin's case.'

Bijan poured two large drinks and came over with them. 'Remember, these are both yours if my man comes in.' And he winked and then pointed at him. 'And yes, that dreadful man. Never liked him, never. Arrogant. Knew his father too.' Bijan cheered and slurped his drink.

Rebwar sipped his whisky. After the initial burn, he soon found some flavours. After years of having to drink whiskies with Bijan, he had slowly appreciated them. This one was peaty and a little bit smoky. West coast he thought.

'What do you think of this one? Talisker from a Scottish island. Thought we were on one.' He laughed. 'Yes, his father left him when he was a teenager. His secretary. I guess Amin learned that lesson well.'

'Yes, my wife too.'

'My poor fellow, if she had come to me... But I heard you were seeing Dinah?' A smile lit up his face.

Rebwar nodded. 'You know where Hourieh is? I need to find her before the police do.'

'All I hear is about you and Dinah and you and Dr Gul. Ah! Yes, and that newsagent. Poor Hussein.'

'Did you know him?'

'Yes, he helped a lot of my friends come here. Have the Turks moved into his territory?'

'Something like that.' Rebwar hadn't the heart to tell him what had happened. He wasn't sure if he would have believed him. 'I heard you still talk to Katarena?'

Bijan put his glass down. 'Dinah tell you that?'

'Yes.'

'Dresses. She wants them so I send them.'

Rebwar got up and took his glass and went over to fill them up again. 'Is she in this country?'

'She was exported.'

'Deported.'

'Yes, yes.'

Rebwar handed him his drink and Bijan gulped it down.

'You think she's here? Go and look, I have nothing to hide... Go, you disgrace me.'

Rebwar didn't want to push any further, as he could also find out in more discreet ways. He knew it wasn't a problem for Bijan to bring Katarena over and keep her in a secret location. 'What if I say that Hourieh is with Katarena?'

'In Kiev?'

'No.'

'So, if you're so clever, go and get her and stop asking me silly questions. You can be an annoying man.'

Rebwar sipped his drink. His cards were on the table.

'So, how is your son?'

'With his mother and I haven't seen him for a couple of months.'

'Good boy you have. Still at school?'

'I think so. He has new friends.'

'Did Hourieh ask for your help to go back to Iran?'

Bijan nodded and rang a bell. His butler came in with a tray of Persian sweets and put them on the table.

'I gave her money for two tickets. I guess she didn't use it.' Bijan stood up and studied what delights were on offer. Rebwar saw something he hadn't seen in a long time: Koloochech, which were little round baked cookies. He grabbed one and let the tastes of cinnamon and crushed walnuts fill his mouth.

Bijan laughed and interlocked his thin bony fingers 'My friend, let's say I tell you...' Bijan leaned in. 'I don't think she will trust me again.'

'I don't understand?'

'The woman, she'll know that you know and that you took her friend away.'

Rebwar now knew, and Bijan now knew that he knew. But how was he going to get her location? And there was a deep mistrust of the police. So in Bijan's eyes, they were safe.

'Who killed Amin?' Bijan said. 'Was it you? I wouldn't blame you.'

'No. I have my suspicions, but Hourieh might know.' Rebwar could see that Bijan was still reserving his judgement on him.

'You are a resourceful man and you know where I stand on the matter. Now tell me about Dinah.'

Rebwar felt embarrassed and didn't want to talk about his affair, as everyone seemed to know about it. 'I will have to leave you, my friend. Someone took those boxes that Amin left here.'

'Oh? Who was it?'

'A man called Dr Norwin, who worked with Amin. They are trying to rescue their business and reputations.'

'By stealing Amin's drugs. People never learn.'

Rebwar was surprised that he knew what was in those boxes and had obviously cared about Dr Gul and must have seen him as a friend. Rebwar said his goodbyes and left.

FORTY-FOUR

Rebwar was sitting outside the Shishwasi and he unfolded his copy of the Hamshahri which he had just bought from one of the local newsagents and flicked over to the sports section. Persepolis had just beaten Paykan two one. It made him feel good as it was an old rival that was originally based in the capital but like nomads had moved around looking for better times. At present they were in the city of Qods in the Tehran province. For a moment he wanted to call Musa to share the news.

Berker brought a small cup of coffee with a little side plate. Rebwar leaned in to have a closer look. It was a kanafeh, which was usually made into cakes, but these looked like mini sausage rolls; made out of vermicelli-like pastry and stuffed with a mixture of nuts, all drenched in rich syrup.

'Ramadan has passed.'

Berker looked around him and took a whole one into his mouth.

'You should get a wife so she can feed you.'

He smiled and walked off. Rebwar carried on reading

the match report. Alipour had scored in the seventy-ninth minute.

'May I?'

Rebwar looked up and saw a man holding onto a chair opposite him. He was short and stocky, wearing a grey suit with a white shirt, which he filled. He had a short trimmed greying beard, a bald head, broken nose and a scar above his thick black eyebrows. Rebwar looked around and saw a couple of free tables.

'Is this chair free?'

The man sat on it. Rebwar looked at him, recognising something familiar about him. He brought out a pack of cigarettes. They were Mehr, which looked like a rip-off of the famous Marlboro pack and was a brand made by the Iranian Tobacco Company – not anyone's choice outside of Iran. The man brought out a matchbox that had the Islamic Republic's flag on it. Rebwar leaned back into his chair, waiting for the man to make his first move.

He inhaled. 'Rebwar, yes?'

Rebwar nodded.

'Difficult man to track down.' He dragged on his cigarette, which had a distinct sharp smell that Rebwar recognised. Then man tapped his index finger on the metal table.

'And you are?'

'Ah, yes, my poor manners.' He presented his right hand to him. 'Esmail Sohrabi. Here you can call me Esmail.' Rebwar leaned in and gave him a firm handshake.

'How do you know me?'

'I am paid to know. How long have you been here?'

'Long enough,' Rebwar waved Berker to come over. 'Coffee?'

Sohrabi nodded and placed a photo on the table which

Rebwar picked up. It was of a man hanging off a construction crane. He'd seen this before. It was a popular form of public execution given out to murderers, rapists, and thieves. He couldn't make out who the man was in the picture. 'Is this a threat?'

'No. Farrouk.'

Rebwar looked at it closer. It could have been him, but he really couldn't tell for sure. Farrouk had been his partner back in Tehran when he was a detective. He had convinced him to go and arrest a local drug lord without clearance from their bosses. Farrouk thought it was an initiative that was going to be rewarded by promotion. He'd always been an insubordinate, flashy idiot that had too much ambition and not enough talent. The operation went south, a child was killed in the crossfire and they both had to disappear before they were going to be made into examples of disobedience. The last he'd heard from Farrouk was in a postcard he had sent to him. Bijan had also mentioned that he had got involved in drug smuggling. Now it looked as if it had all caught up with him.

'And you came all the way here to tell me?'

'No, I'm looking into Dr Amin Gul.' He drew hard on his cigarette, which had burned unevenly.

Berker came back with two coffees, put them down and left. He knew the likes of Sohrabi. As a Kurd, he'd seen more of them than he cared for.

'What's up with the Kurd?'

'You know he's dead?'

'Dr Gul? Don't make me laugh. Remember I can pay for a lot of things. And you expect this country to protect you.' He lit another cigarette, puffing away and blowing its tip to make sure it smouldered.

'What do you want?'

Sohrabi played with his matchbox by sliding his fingers from one end to the other and upturning it on the table. 'I see you like this.' And he took out a match and showed it to him. 'Small little man with a fiery head and I can, at any time do this.' He lit the match and relit his cigarette. 'Now, tell me about Dr Gul.'

'Eminent plastic surgeon. Had a good practice close to Harley Street and made some money on the side selling opioids, which got him killed.'

Sohrabi crossed his legs and tapped his cigarette on the ashtray. 'I think there was a lot more. How did you know him?'

'Friend of a friend of my wife's and I didn't know him.'

Sohrabi wagged his index finger at him. 'All you refugees know each other. Rats like to hang around each other. I will find out, remember that. Now if you have anything else to say, do contact me.'

'And how would I do that?'

'Ask Bijan. He knows where to find me.'

'Hey, Rebs, you're looking good, my love.' Rebwar looked over to see Tamar, who was a friend of his and had helped him with a few cases. She had worked as a stripper in Soho and was now a webcam girl and occasional belly dancer in the local restaurants. She was as glamorous as usual, wearing tight-fitting leggings, and a red Puma tracksuit top that was unzipped to show off her deep cleavage. She had dyed her hair blonde and had thick red lips. She leaned in to kiss his cheek making sure they both had a good look at her.

'Oh, sorry forgot,' Tamar rubbed the lipstick mark off his cheek and giggled. 'Just can't help myself. So who's your friend?'

'He—'

'Colonel Esmail Sohrabi. Pleasure to meet you, Tamar.'

Tamar fluttered her large eyebrows. 'A colonel, I'm honoured, sir. From the same homeland?' She pointed at them both.

'Yes, my dear, I was catching up with Mr Ghorbani here.'

'So, you work for the military? Big guns and command men?'

Rebwar offered her a cigarette. Sohrabi leaned in with his pack. 'Oh, look, they look interesting.' She took one of the Mehr cigarettes. Rebwar wanted to warn her but refrained as he didn't want to embarrass Sohrabi. He was one of those typical proud bureaucrats who loved to act on petty revenges. As Sohrabi struck the match he looked over at Rebwar and smiled.

Tamar leaned in. 'You look like one of those...' She drew hard on the cigarette. Sohrabi licked his lips as he watched her. She coughed. 'Crikey... Yeah, special...' She looked at the pack. 'SAVAK yes? James Bond.'

Sohrabi smiled. 'Just a colonel.'

'So what brings you to Britain? Buying some weapons, like some big guns. Sure you've got plenty of them.' She giggled.

Rebwar watched Sohrabi and enjoyed seeing him being slowly disarmed by his lust.

'My dear, I couldn't possibly give you that kind of information. I would have to kill you for it.' For the first time, he laughed and revealed his yellowing teeth.

'You have some nice friends, Rebs.' Tamar put her arm around Rebwar and grabbed his arm to put it around her waist. 'How long are you staying? Maybe you can stay around to watch me dance.'

'Only a few days, I have some meetings. When is the show?'

'I have one tonight and tomorrow. Sure, I can make a special show for you, Colonel. Now, I have to get ready for tonight.' She kissed Rebwar's cheek and grabbed Sohrabi's hand and kissed it. 'Lovely to meet you, Colonel, Uh, sounds so sexy – Colonel.' And she walked off.

Both watched her swing her broad, round backside. In acknowledgement, she turned around and blew a kiss at them.

Sohrabi laughed. He turned to face Rebwar and his face dropped back to his interrogative look. 'Mr Ghorbani.' He picked up the spent match. 'Remember, Dr Amin Gul.' He got up and said his goodbyes and left.

Berker came to clear the table. 'You know that man?'

Rebwar shook his head.

'Government?'

'Yep, probably VAJA. Think Amin was expanding his network and he had appeared on their radar.'

FORTY-FIVE

Geraldine had just presented her warrant card to one of her colleagues at the door of KhanWin Beauty. She'd heard from Tim Carpenter that there had been a serious incident in a medical practice close to Harley Street. Carpenter kept an open live feed of the Met police on his PC. He tried to live his cop fantasies over them, pretending to know what had happened. This one had caught Geraldine's attention and she hoped that she had beaten DS Hunter to the scene. She went up to a uniformed WPC. 'Who called it?'

The officer turned to her. Striking blue eyes, short bob and Asian skin. 'The cleaner.' Her radio handset crackled, and she responded by telling control that they were still waiting for DS Hunter and SOCO.

'Has she been interviewed?'

The officer shook her head. Geraldine spotted the cleaner sitting on a chair in the waiting room. She went over. 'Hi, I'm DS Smith. Can I ask you a few questions?'

'I'm Marian.' She pointed to herself. She was short and brown-skinned with thin straight hair. 'Me no speak good English.'

'Where did you find her?'

'In toilet. Disgusting.' She held her mouth with her hand. 'She dead? Never seen dead.'

'Did you know her?'

'A little. She nice girl. Always... how do say?' And she smiled and held it.

'Happy?'

'Yes, happy. So sad, sad now.'

'Is she usually here when you clean?'

Marian looked back at her. 'I only clean one time now. Very little.'

Geraldine had spotted that and had guessed that, since her last visit, Dr Norwin had scheduled a clean.

'Did you see anyone else? Or something odd?'

'Yes, no rubbish. I take rubbish out and... no. All gone.'

Out of breath and flustered, Dr Norwin walked into the reception. Geraldine went over to Ms Maddox's body which lay slumped next to the toilet. One of her arms lay draped over the seat with a needle and syringe. She found it a little off. It didn't feel like suicide and if it was an overdose then why? Ss she must have had some knowledge of drugs as well as having aspirations, as she had told Rebwar. When Beckie overdosed and that was a cry for help and she wanted to be found. She couldn't have known that Marian was coming by. She heard Dr Norwin shout out. 'No!' as he tried to make his way to the scene. Geraldine went over to see him.

'DS Smith... what happened?'

'Too early to say and waiting for SOCO to process the scene.'

'Suicide? She was... Oh God.' Dr Norwin bit into his clenched fist.

'Be best if we went to your office.'

In his office, which was clean, Dr Norwin slumped into one of the couches by the shelves with the medical books.

'Dr Norwin, did Ms Maddox have a known drug addiction?'

'No, no, I mean people do and... but no. Do you think it had anything to do with Dr Khan?'

'What? You think that...' Dr Norwin looked blankly into the grey carpeted floor. 'Oh, the poor girl. I told him not to. He has a weakness for women. He's a sex addict, and I have told him to go and get some therapy for it. Damned idiot.'

'What were you doing at Bijan Achmoud's house?'

'Sorry, who?'

'General Achmoud. You were seen there.'

'Uh, well, I was picking up a package. It was Dr Gul's. He left it there.'

'What was it?'

'Some medicines for the practice. We stored it there.' Dr Norwin wiped his forehead.

'It was a Poroxy package, wasn't it? The ones that Dr Gul was selling on the black market.'

'No, you're not getting the bigger picture. We were taking them back to Poroxy. Cleaning up his mess.'

'Not the story I heard.'

'DS Smith, you don't strike me as a woman who would succumb to gossip.'

'Where's Dr Khan?'

'I'm not sure, I have left a message for him.'

'Saying?'

'To come here!'

'And Ms Boyd have you contacted her?'

'Yes, same message.'

Geraldine pulled up one of the chairs and sat on it.

'Should I call my lawyer?'

'That's up to you. Can you tell me what happened between Ms Maddox and Dr Khan?'

'Yes, uh... no, sorry. I think it best that I get legal advice.'

Geraldine leaned back. 'Yeah, I understand. But what I don't understand is why Ms Maddox would commit suicide here? At home, I would get it. But here? Somewhere where she's probably had a traumatic experience. To me, it makes no sense. But to you as a doctor...'

Dr Norwin looked towards the door and the frosted glass wall. Outline shapes passed it. 'Sorry, yes, yes.' Dr Norwin scratched the back of his head. His phone rang, and he picked up. 'Vivek, yes I am... OK, and you're...'

Geraldine signalled to Dr Khan to pass over the phone, which he did. 'DS Smith. Dr Khan are you on your way here?'

'DS Smith, I am yes.'

'You coming from home?'

'Yes, yes.'

'I'll meet you there. This is a crime scene and we need to clear it. What is your home address?' He told her and Geraldine wrote it down on a pad on the desk. 'Stay there till I arrive.'

'Shouldn't he be going to the police station?' said Dr Norwin.

DS Hunter burst into the office with another officer. 'DS Smith, what a... surprise.'

'DS Hunter, he's all yours. I was making sure he wasn't going to contaminate the crime scene.'

'Crime... Yes, thank you, DS Smith. Good thinking.' DS Hunter walked over to Geraldine and in a lowered voice said. 'I'll be having words.'

Geraldine walked out then came back to pick up the

note she had written. Time was ticking before DS Hunter was going to bring in Dr Khan. She also had to get Rebwar to talk to Ms Boyd. She felt they were getting close as the killer had struck again. She went up to the WPC she had talked to and said, 'Has anyone looked at the CCTV?'

'It's been wiped clean. First thing I checked, ma'am.'

Geraldine looked around the reception area. 'So what made you check the CCTV?'

'Wanted to check that the cleaner hadn't fibbed. Could have been a robbery.'

'Good. Good work.' And Geraldine went over to the lift.

FORTY-SIX

Rebwar was in Dinah's boutique on King's Road smoking and watching her assistant, Aza, sew a button on a long flowing dress. Raj sat eating a doughnut.

'And there's a battery in there?' asked Rebwar.

'Uncle, we've used them before. Just looks like a button.' Raj brought out his phone and showed him a blue dot on a map. 'Look, working.'

Rebwar tapped his cigarette on the ashtray. Dinah walked in and looked at the scene.

'Finished yet? I need to work here.'

Aza looked up.

Rebwar said, 'Can I get another coffee...' and added, 'my love.' Her face lit up and she smiled. She turned around and with a little swinging rhythm walked off. Rebwar pondered for a moment, letting it sink in that what would normally be a throwaway remark, felt more of a declaration of his feelings. He looked over to Raj, who was trying to contain his giggle.

'Aza, when is the courier coming?'

She looked up from her sewing and checked her watch. 'In twenty minutes.'

'Good, good. And she won't notice that we've changed those buttons?'

Dinah came back in with an espresso. 'Rebwar, it's a present. She never sees them, and neither does Bijan. They have no idea. I could send them a dress made out of tea towels and they wouldn't know.'

Rebwar looked at the dress, it was long, deep and silky blue, with a string of precious stones running down on each side. For a moment he wanted Dinah to try it on for him.

She handed him the espresso and whispered into his ear. 'I've got one at home. You can't wear any underwear.' She kissed his neck and his arm reacted with goosebumps.

'Bit chilly here,' He downed the espresso, looked at his phone, and noticed a message for him. It was from Geraldine and she wanted him to interview Llaria Boyd. 'I'm going to have to go.'

Aza and Raj said their goodbyes and Dinah led Rebwar out to the front of the closed shop. She opened the door, grabbed his cheeks, and kissed him. He didn't want to go but spent this moment with her. It was as delicious as one of her *Bamieh*[1] pastries.

———

He was standing in front of the Boswell Residences in Holborn, which was an old, brick building down a little stone-paved alley that connected Boswell Street and New N Street. He looked up at tall sash windows, a couple of which had lights on. A series of Victorian-style street lights lit the surrounding council apartment blocks. The facade had been painted dark blue and white. Rebwar called Geraldine.

'I'm here. What am I asking?'

'What her movements were. We've found Attesa Maddox dead in the KhanWin toilet.'

Rebwar let that sink in for a moment. She had helped them break into the practice and had been kind and caring. 'What happened?'

'Not sure. Looks like a suicide, but I'm not convinced.'

'How?'

'Overdose. I'm not buying it and I'm confronting Dr Khan.'

'Alone?'

'I've got my CS spray.'

'Can't it wait?'

'No, DS Hunter is on my heels and I don't want him to fuck this up. I'll call you later.'

Rebwar went up to the entrance door and buzzed Ms Boyd's flat.

'Hello,' came a faint voice.

'I'm here to see Ms Boyd.'

'She is not here. Sorry.'

Rebwar noticed that the voice was almost musical. 'I have a package for her, can I come in to drop it off?' And the door buzzed open.

Rebwar got to the second floor where a tall blonde woman waited by the door. 'Hi, I'm Rebwar,' The door was on its security latch and he could only see half her face. He slipped in his business card.

'Malin,' She read his card. 'You are a private investigator? Why do you not just call her? Is she in trouble?'

'I've tried. She is in danger. One of her work colleagues got murdered.'

She stepped back and covered her mouth with her hands.

'Look, you sure she's not here? I need to find her.'

'Oh, she goes bowling every Wednesday and Friday. She's very crazy for it.'

'I've just checked there,' Rebwar lied. 'Would you mind if I can see her room? She might have left some clues. I hope nothing has happened to her.'

'You think she is in danger? Have you called the police?'

'I work for the police.'

She looked at his card. 'I call you if she comes.'

'Does she have a boyfriend?'

Malin shook her head.

'An ex?'

'He died. Sad story.' She flicked her blonde hair off her pretty face.

Rebwar leaned on the hallway wall. 'What happened?'

'He was in an accident and never recovered. She was very sad.'

'Do you know his name?'

'Aahil. Nice man. He was a cook.'

'Persian name. Was he from Iran like me?'

She smiled. 'Yes, yes nice smile like yours...' She looked down.

'When did this happen?'

'Couple of years ago.'

The front door opened and footsteps echoed up the stairwell. Rebwar looked back and waited. He guessed by their weight and rhythm that it could be a woman. Out of the shadows, a woman appeared wearing a black hijab, her face covered by the veil.

Rebwar said, '*Salām, asr bekheir.*[2]'

The woman just nodded and carried on up the stairs.

Rebwar noticed that she was carrying a black leather holdall and Nike trainers. 'Neighbour?'

In a hushed voice, Malin said. 'Big Arab community here. Not friendly.'

'Arabs...' Rebwar shrugged. 'Different... nice meeting you, Malin.'

Malin undid the latch. 'I know I shouldn't. Maybe crazy. But if this helps you to find Llaria. I let you see her room.'

'Thank you, Malin. If it'll make you feel better, leave the door open and stand here.'

Rebwar passed her and went inside where there was a clean and sparse sitting room with a TV, an armchair, two-seater sofa, a coffee table, and some generic pictures of landscapes. Rebwar looked back at Malin, who was still standing by the open door. 'Llaria's room?'

'End.' She gave a thumbs up.

Rebwar opened the door and switched the light on. He took photos of the room which had a double bed with a flowery cover and cushions, a wardrobe with mirrored doors and a chest of drawers. Beside her bed was a medium-sized bag with a pair of bowling shoes. He opened it and found two bowling balls. Dotted around the furniture were some pictures, which Rebwar picked up. A couple of them had a picture of a young man. He guessed it must have been Aahil. Rebwar opened the wardrobe where there were a couple of dresses and suits. He checked their labels and they were of high street brands: Whistles, Reiss and M&S. Behind the door was a leather case. Inside, he found a small laptop and took it out. He lifted the back of his jacket and slipped it under his belt. He checked himself in the mirror.

He went up to Malin. 'Thank you, it was a great help.

She hasn't changed bowling alley? I might have got the wrong one.'

'I think it's the one around the corner. All Star Lanes.'

'Thank you, been a great help. I will find her.'

Rebwar called Raj and told him to meet him at All Star Lanes, which was around the corner in Victoria House, a huge imposing building that looked like it could have housed a bank or a government department. He walked around it looking for the entrance. There was a small park in front of it and large townhouses faced it. On one of the corners, he spotted a neon sign that led into the basement. The place looked like an American Diner with booths and four bowling lanes. It was busy with a lot of men and women wearing their city suits. A waitress in a tight-fitting white T-shirt and a mini skirt asked if he was looking for a table. Her look fitted in with the sixties decor with its mint coloured vinyl seats and neon signs.

Rebwar chose one of the booths and waited for Raj to come by. He glanced around hoping to see Ms Boyd, but as she had left her bowling gear she was probably somewhere else. He was hoping to find out more from her laptop, which he'd laid next to him on the seat. The place was popular with groups celebrating birthdays or work events. A few of them were ordering shots and daring each other. Rebwar didn't dwell on their games and kept scanning for Raj.

'Uncle.'

Rebwar turned around to see Raj. He was wearing a large grey and dark blue T-shirt with a crest of the NFL.

'Is that some bowling team?'

Raj slid himself across, nearly filling up both spaces. 'It's American Football. Thought it would fit in... sort of.' He picked up the menu. 'Burgers. Nice one, Uncle.'

'Rebwar grabbed it off him. Work first, then rewards.' He put the laptop on the table.

Raj whistled and opened it up. 'Mac. Where did you get this one?'

'Can you crack it?'

Raj powered it on and looked around as he waited. 'How did you find this place?'

Rebwar pointed at the computer.

'You nicked it here?'

'The suspect comes here.'

Raj turned it around to show him the screen. 'Done...'

'How?'

'She didn't have a password. What are we looking for?'

'You sure?' Raj nodded. 'Emails. Look for a guy called Aahil. It was her boyfriend.'

Raj clicked around the screen; windows opened and closed. He tutted to himself and slowly increased to swearing.

'She didn't put a password?'

'No. Shitty Mac. It's like an annoying expensive children's toy.'

'It's a computer, no?'

Raj rocked his head from side to side. 'Yeah but it's like

the English and the French. They like to do things differently and it's annoying.'

'Stop with your colonial conspiracies. Is he in there?'

'Hi, guys, what can I do for you?'

They both stared at a smiling, dark-haired waitress. She was chewing gum and had plump lips that had seen a little too much filler. Rebwar clicked his fingers at Raj to get his attention.

'Yeah, the kingpin, well done, skinny fries,' to which he giggled. 'House slaw and buffalo wings. And a large Coke.'

'Sure. And you, sir?'

'Is the Pacifico beer similar to the Corona?'

'Yes, it is.'

Rebwar lifted his index finger.

'And to eat?'

'I'll have some of his fries.'

Raj said, 'Two portions, then.'

And she turned around and walked off, swinging her hips. Raj kept staring till Rebwar flicked his ear.

'Hey! OK, OK, slave driver. Never get paid enough for this. You know that.' Raj kept typing as he spoke. 'Hey, how about a computer course? Government will pay you... No?'

Rebwar kept looking around, hoping to spot something. 'Hey, you keep digging. I'm going to ask around and have a cigarette. Also, look for Dr Khan. Something went on between them.'

Raj kept typing and clicking and shaking his head. Rebwar knew he was off into that digital world, which he himself refused to learn. Next to the booths were four bowling lanes with a bar facing them. He went over to it and sat on one of the stools. A barman waited on him. He asked for another Pacifico beer.

'Thanks, I'm looking for Llaria?' The man shrugged and Rebwar showed a picture of her.

The bartender put on his glasses. 'Yeah, she plays here.'

'And today?'

'No.'

Rebwar took a sip of his beer. 'Are any of her friends here?'

The bartender pointed at a group playing on the first lane. Rebwar thanked him and went over to them. There were three of them, two men and a woman. Rebwar approached one of the men who was sitting down. He was tall and dark-haired with strong eyebrows, a square jaw, and wore dungarees.

'Hi, I'm looking for Llaria.'

'Hey, man, you a friend?' The man looked up.

'Colleague. Heard I could find her here.'

'She's not here today.'

'Do you know where I can find her?'

The man leaned back and ran his finger through his thick hair. 'Tried calling her?'

Rebwar nodded. 'Heard she's quite dedicated. Odd, no?'

The man frowned. 'What's with the questions?'

'Oh, I have some urgent work information to pass on.'

'Really? Can I help?'

'You know where she is?'

The man looked at a strike that one of the women had bowled. He raised his beer at her. 'No, I don't but I'll mention it if I see her. What work you do?'

'Supplier.'

'OK. Your name is?'

'Rebwar, I need to see her.'

The man got up, went up to the ball dispenser and

chose one. Rebwar watched him bowl. He got all the pins bar one.

Rebwar returned to Raj who had already eaten his burger. 'Found anything?'

'Uncle, you need to sit down.' He wiped his brow. 'There's some bad shit. Amin, man!'

Rebwar ordered another two beers.

'Aahil was involved in a hit and run a couple of years ago, and that's how Llaria met Amin. He tried to fix him but his injuries were so bad that he got hooked on painkillers... Yeah, fucked up and Amin provided him with Poroxy. But the shit got darker. He ended up on heroin and overdosed. Llaria took it bad and kind of blackmailed herself into working for Amin and KhanWin.'

'Blackmailed?'

'She was studying,' Raj checked the computer. 'Anaesthetist... the ones that put you to sleep. She said wanted a job at KhanWin otherwise she'd sue him for malpractice.'

'She got what she wanted... OK and Dr Khan?'

'Yeah, he tried it on with her and she sued him.'

'Anything else?'

'Yeah, looks like they were having money problems. Amin left and both of them stopped paying her – or initially less and recently nothing.' Raj showed him some emails. 'She was pissed off.'

Geraldine had taken a cab to the address that Dr Khan had given, which was up in Harrow in North London. The black cab pulled onto Broadfields, which was a road just off Headstone overground train station. She had to guide the cabbie to the exact spot as his 'knowledge' only dealt with central London and not the commuter belt. They stopped at what looked like a house that had been made out of four or five differently-sized sections. By the number of parking spaces, she guessed that it had been divided into apartments. The building faced out onto a park. She paid the cab driver, who wished her luck and drove off. As the diesel engine droned off, an eerie silence took over. A few lights lit the parking and common areas of the modern brick building. She saw Dr Khan's blue Porsche that Rebwar had mentioned.

At the back of the apartment block was the entrance with a series of flat numbers. She pressed Number Six and waited then rang it again. She then tried his phone but there was no answer. She walked off around the property to see if there was a light on in his flat. At the front, facing the park, was what looked like a shared garden, which had a railing blocking the access. A light caught her attention, flickering through the bare trees and shrubs along the line of houses that faced the open green space. She could smell smoke – not wood or coal, but something a bit more chemical. She tried to call again but just got Dr Khan's voicemail.

According to her phone's map, the fire was a bit further down Broadfields and into Headstone Lane. Out of curiosity and a hunch, she decided to head over there. After a few minutes, she got to the Blue Room Sports Venue, which looked like a large clubhouse but had been orphaned of whatever game it had been associated with. She could now see the smoke drifting over the empty field and it was coming from the back of one of the houses just across from where she was standing. She walked across the grass, being careful not to trip in a rabbit hole. She looked over the hedge and saw a man burning a pile of cardboard boxes.

Flames flickered up as he added another empty box to the bonfire. As the fire took hold of the cardboard, she saw Dr Khan's face. He was burning the evidence. She saw a small wooden gate and reached over and opened the latch.

'Dr Khan, stop.'

He looked over and tried to work out who it was.

'Dr Khan, it's over. Stop and raise your hands?'

'DS Smith, it's all a misunderstanding. I'm helping my ex-wife clear up.'

Geraldine got her handcuffs out.

'No, not here, please. Not in front of my children. I'll do whatever you ask.'

'Dr Khan, put your hands behind your head.'

The back door opened and Dr Khan's wife walked over

to them. She was a short, stocky woman in a knee-length dress and leggings.

'What is going on here?'

'Mrs Khan, I am detaining your husband.'

'Do you have the authority?'

'Yes, Mrs Khan, I am a police officer.' Geraldine produced her warrant card and showed it to her.

'And an arrest warrant or some legal document?'

'Mrs Khan, please go back into the house. This does not concern you.'

She stepped in between them. 'He's my ex-husband and it doesn't concern me? Now get off my property and he'll answer your questions tomorrow.'

'Mrs Khan, please, you making yourself an accessory to murder.'

She looked over to Dr Khan, who shook his head. 'What right have you to accuse my ex-husband of murder in front of his family and neighbours. I am not moving from here.' She crossed her arms.

Geraldine walked around to Dr Khan and Mrs Khan blocked her. 'I will have to arrest you both and call social services. You don't want that.'

'You get out of my garden. I am not having anyone come here and just arrest my ex-husband and violate his human rights.'

Geraldine pushed Mrs Khan out of the way, grabbed Dr Khan's left arm and secured one of the cuffs. Mrs Khan hit Geraldine's arm and screamed. In turn, Geraldine pushed her and she fell on the grass close to the fire. Geraldine secured the second cuff on Dr Khan's right arm, and now both arms were behind his back. Lights came on in the neighbouring houses and two kids appeared by the patio, their faces frozen with shock. In her raging anger, Mrs Khan picked up the end of a smouldering piece of cardboard and threw it at Geraldine.

'Stay back,' Geraldine held her mace spray and pointed it at Mrs Khan. 'I will use it. Keep away.'

Mrs Khan kicked another empty box at her and grabbed another one beside her. Geraldine's thumb pressed the canister's button and a jet of white mist engulfed Mrs Khan, now blindly lashing out. She swung the box wildly and in her frenzy, it landed on the fire; she held onto it as it caught alight, her eyes bloodshot and streaming. With her free hand, she raged and tried to wipe and rub her face. And kept swinging the now flaming box around her.

'Let go of the box,' said Geraldine.

Which she did. The box hurtled at Dr Khan, who was unable to use his arms to protect himself. Panicked, he desperately tried to free himself. The box hit him squarely on his chest. He stumbled backwards and lost his balance and fell heavily onto his back. The burning box clung to him like an octopus engulfing its prey. Desperate screams turned to high-pitched cries for help as Dr Khan rolled and kicked out. Geraldine took off her bomber jacket and tried to put the fire out.

'Someone get an extinguisher, now!'

Mrs Khan kept hitting Geraldine. Fists and kicks landed on her face, legs and body. Geraldine tried to hold her back. 'Mrs Khan, your husband is on fire.'

One of the boys came running out of the house with an extinguisher and Geraldine ran over to get it. Her training took over and she pulled the pin, aimed, squeezed the handle and swept from side to side till the fire was out. Mrs Khan slumped over facing her groaning ex-husband. And it was then that Geraldine noticed sirens and flashing lights around her. Officers, firemen and paramedics rushed around her.

'Are you all right?' Geraldine nodded, trying to catch her breath, pain spots appearing like dropping rain. She knelt down, her senses returning.

FORTY-NINE

Rebwar was in his kitchen reading an old edition of the Hamshahri, a popular Tehran newspaper, with a cup of sweet black coffee and a cigarette. It was the usual old stories of US sanctions, rising oil prices and an attack on an Iranian military parade where twenty-nine soldiers had been killed. The government blamed the US for sponsoring terrorism. He flicked through to find some football stories. He heard light footsteps walking down the staircase and Alanza walked into the kitchen. Wearing only Genny's Brazilian football top, she smiled shyly and tried to shape her unruly curly hair.

'Hey,' she said, opening the fridge.

'Morning.'

'Can I get a drag?'

'Sure.'

She puffed a couple of times before smiling again and got the milk out.

'I'd check.'

She opened and smelled it. 'Glass?'

Rebwar pointed at a cupboard next to the sink and

watched her bare feet as she reached for the shelf. She poured herself a glass of milk.

'There's coffee on the stove if you want to take some to Genny. He has two sugars.'

'Thanks, they're sleeping...'

Rebwar looked up and realised. She stood gulping down her milk. He handed her a cigarette and she held up two fingers. Rebwar gave her another two and she returned upstairs. He smiled and couldn't wait to tell Dinah. His phone rang. It was Raj.

'Uncle, the package has left Bijan's house and I'm tracking. It's going east – just past the city and heading towards the docklands.'

Rebwar stood up and took his keys, cigarettes, lighter, and wallet and put on his black leather jacket.

By the time the tracker had stopped, Rebwar was getting off a bus close to Poplar station. Raj had worked out that the package had been delivered to New Providence Wharf, which was a new apartment development in Canary Wharf.

'Take either the D6 or D7 bus,' Raj had said.

'Do you know which apartment number?'

'No. All I can see is that the building is like a horseshoe and faces onto the river. I think it's still at the reception.'

Rebwar had got onto the D7 double-decker bus, which took him to the Poplar Waterside & Marina, which was obstructed by a high brick wall, and got off opposite at Aspen Way stop. He walked down St Lawrence Street, a mish-mash of boxy modern houses, a couple of old cottages and contemporary apartment blocks. He got to the end where blocks of flats towered in front of him. Raj guided him to the reception area, which was off a roundabout and up towards the Radisson Hotel, the tallest building of the complex.

He arrived in a sparse-looking reception space with a small waiting area. On the other side were a man and woman standing behind a large wooden desk. He went up to the man who was bald and wearing a high-vis jacket over his black suit.

'Looking for a Mrs Ghorbani.'

'Got an apartment number?'

He shook his head and the man typed into his keyboard. 'No one under that name. You can call them and they can buzz you in.'

Rebwar called Raj and walked over to the waiting area. 'Is the package where I am?'

'Uncle, it's not that accurate but I think so. It's not in the water or in the dome.'

'Dome?'

'Millennial Dome, it's opposite. The O2...' Raj sighed. 'I'll call you when it moves.'

Rebwar sat down on one of the chairs in the reception. He didn't know what he was going to say to Hourieh or how she was going to react. Badly, he thought. The last time they had broken up was in Tehran when Musa was born. Hourieh had gone home to her parents to have him. Rebwar had argued that she should have gone to a hospital. But it was tradition to have a home birth, or in her family it was and he couldn't afford it. Having nurses and a midwife. This also made it all the more difficult, as the police precinct was on the other side of town. It meant he was only back home for a couple of hours, which upset her family, each one having a go at his dead-end job. The joke was that he was the least corrupt out of all of them. And of course, he missed the birth and only saw his son the day after. Hourieh made sure he could only see him during the weekends and he had to stay at their apartment.

He saw a tall thin blonde woman in sunglasses, a short light blue jacket with silver trim along the edges, a matching short skirt, red high heels and gold bangles on her wrists. Rebwar looked down, hoping not to be noticed. It was Katarena Kostova, Bijan's fiancée. As suspected, she was in the country.

'You have package?'

'Name?'

'Mrs Achmoud.'

The security woman opened a door behind the desk and fetched the package. Rebwar recognised it as the parcel that Dinah had sent to Bijan.

'Nice present, going somewhere nice?' said the woman, handing over the box.

'Can you deliver?'

'Sure, Mrs Achmoud, I can help take it upstairs if you like,' said the man.

Rebwar got up and hid by an alcove with a large plant and watched them call for a lift. It stopped on the eighteenth floor. He looked over to see if the woman was watching him, but she was on a call looking out onto the road and he called the second elevator. Once there, he admired the thickly carpeted corridor, which was lined with flower arrangements. Their scent drifted to give a warm welcome. There was nowhere he could hide, so he kept the lift doors open and waited. He heard a door open, followed by the man's voice.

'Thank you so much, Mrs Achmoud. I shall make sure, yes, yes.'

Rebwar noted the door from which he came out and returned to the lift and went two floors down. He waited for a minute to go back to the floor. He walked up to the door and tried to listen in. There was some music, but no sounds of Musa or Hourieh. He was having doubts about her being there.

FIFTY

Geraldine sat on the windowsill in her tank top and knickers smoking a cigarette and blowing out the smoke through the half-opened sash. She looked down on the street, watching the morning rush of commuters setting off to their offices. Images still flashed of Dr Khan's desperate attempts to smother the fire. She hadn't slept much, instead, fighting with her aching injuries and the knowledge that they still hadn't found the killer. Dr Khan had been put in an induced coma and they had now to wait to talk to him. She stubbed her cigarette in between the other cigarettes.

'Hey G, light me one.'

Geraldine looked over to her bed where Sandra was stretching her arms out. She had been glad to find her home last night, although she still didn't know how she felt about her. They still hadn't had a conversation about their past or what she did for a living. All she really knew was that she was twenty-four, liked to taste new adventures, and would like to have a sunset cocktail over the Pacific followed by sunrise on the Indian ocean with coffee and cigarettes. You have to dream to get. And that was her dating profile with a few sexy photos.

She got off the window ledge and saw herself in the mirror. Her legs and arms were bruised from Mrs Khan's fists and kicks.

'Have you taken the arnica I gave you?'

Geraldine looked over at her night table. No, she hadn't. Instead, she got another pack of cigarettes and passed one to Sandra.

'So you got beaten up by some brown bitch. How's she looking?'

'I maced her.'

'You should have punched her lights out.' Sandra propped herself up on the headboard and flicked her blonde hair off her T-shirt, which had text saying, Let's get one thing straight, I'm not.

'Didn't fancy a suspension. Although we could have had some duvet days.'

Sandra lifted her left eyebrow and winked. 'I can call?'

'Yeah, uh, I know it's a weird question but what do you do?'

Sandra laughed and hid half her face with the duvet. 'I'm a part-time barista and a stripper.' And she hid her face under the duvet.

'Fuck off... you're lying about being a—'

'Barista, yes...'

'Fuck me sideways. I'm going out with a stripper!'

———

Geraldine's phone rang. It was Rebwar. 'Hey, Rebs.'

'You're in a good mood?'

'Yeah, yeah, what's up?'

'I've got Hourieh's location and I'm going to see her. I need to find out what she saw on the night. Did you get anything out of Dr Khan?'

Geraldine rubbed her neck and felt her bruises twitch with pain. 'He's in a coma. His ex managed to set him on fire. Long story – and we have to wait till he wakes to know more.'

'I don't think it's him. I went to see Ms Boyd, but she wasn't in. We need to check her alibi for yesterday.'

'OK, I'm on my way.' She hung up and looked over at Sandra. 'Am I going to have to install a pole?'

———

Geraldine pressed on Ms Boyd's buzzer at the Boswell Residences but no answer came. She tried the other flats and found one that was occupied and she used her police credentials. The door opened, and on the way up a woman peeked out of her front door. Geraldine showed her warrant and thanked her. She got to Ms Boyd's flat and tried to open the door. It was locked and she banged on the door with her fist. No response. She kneeled down, flipped the letterbox flap and peered in. There was a woman on the floor in a pool of blood. Geraldine stood up and took out her phone. In her panic, it slipped out of her hands and fell. The screen had cracked but she managed to call for help.

Five police officers had been dispatched to help, and they had brought the enforcer with them – or 'the big red key' as they liked to call it. The officer used the big red ram to break the door down and ran in to check on the woman. The officer confirmed that there was a pulse and the paramedics went in to treat her. Geraldine saw that it wasn't Ms

Boyd but her flatmate Malin, The blood trailed to a corner of the room where a bowling ball lay.

Geraldine went into Ms Boyd's bedroom. It looked like it had been ransacked. Was it a burglary that had gone wrong? She took photos of the room. On top of a dresser was a little decorative plate with some jewellery. Geraldine snapped a picture and found some more little boxes holding rings and earrings. The wardrobe and drawers had been opened and emptied on the floor. There were blouses, socks, knickers, bras, jumpers and jeans. In a corner was a pile of laundry and she noticed a black fabric. She picked it up and laid it out on the floor and took a picture. It was a burka. There was no sign of a struggle or fight in the bedroom. She went back into the living room to find that the paramedics had taken Malin away. Police officers were processing the scene, collecting evidence. It was only a matter of time till DS Hunter would be called in. But she wasn't going to help them connect the dots. She had to find Ms Boyd and determine if she had done this or she was being chased. But by whom? They were running out of suspects. Dr Norwin had been taken into custody by DS Hunter; Dr Khan was in hospital, and Buckham was dead. And then there was Jim Jacobi who had been picked up at his house but later released.

A SOCO team arrived at the flat and they were told to leave. It was now out of her hands and it would a day or two before she heard or saw a report unless DS Hunter put an emergency order on it. But that wasn't going to happen, especially if she asked him. Geraldine selected some pictures of the scene and sent them to Rebwar.

FIFTY-ONE

Rebwar stood outside Katarena's front door, hesitating to knock, not knowing what he was going to find out, not knowing how Musa was doing, not knowing how Hourieh was going to react. They needed to talk, argue, shout, cry and listen to each other. It wasn't all going to happen. He wanted to blame it all on Dr Amin Gul but that was the easy way out. He was dead. How was he going to answer back? Rebwar knocked three times on the door and waited, listening out for voices. Katarena opened the door and waited for Rebwar to say something.

'Hi, Katarena.'

'How you find me?'

'Are my wife and son here?'

'No?'

But Musa walked out into the large living room behind her. He looked older, with neatly combed hair and dressed in a blue shirt and khaki shorts. 'Father!' And he ran over to him and hugged him.

Hourieh appeared. 'What's going on?'

She was dressed in a yellow and red patterned silk

blouse, black skirt, bangles and her usual trinkets. Her black hair was tied up and she looked younger. Rebwar was taken back to when they were living in Tehran and used to go out to dinner parties. She would hold court with the men, making them smoke cigars, flatter them and ask when her husband would be getting a promotion. The colonel's daughter, who charmed old men.

'Husband, what are you doing here? You must—'

'Mum,' Musa tapped Rebwar's chest. 'I want to go to McDonald's and have a flurry.'

Katarena walked away back into the apartment.

'Don't call Bijan,' said Hourieh. 'I will deal with this.'

'Ten minutes, I told you.'

'And I told you he would find us.'

'My desert flower, I must talk to you. Coffee?' Rebwar didn't dare to go in and waited patiently for her to make a decision.

'I can't, can I?' She held her forehead. 'I have to stay away, understand?'

'No, I don't. I need to know what happened that night. A woman has been killed and another one is in hospital. Were you here last night?'

'No she wasn't,' said Musa.

'Where?'

Hourieh looked away and crossed her arms. Rebwar grabbed her shoulders. 'Look at me. I don't care if you were seeing another man... OK, I do, but it's... complicated. I still love you and want to see my son. But I need to know that you weren't involved in his accident or murder.'

She turned around and with her dark eyes looked at him. 'No.'

'What no?'

'No, I wasn't there. No, I didn't kill him. No, I don't want to tell you.'

Musa grabbed Rebwar's jacket. 'Dad, Dad, we can go along the river and talk. Like you always say to me, a new perspective brings a new viewpoint.'

Rebwar looked at his son. 'You're so grown up, my boy.' He turned to Hourieh. 'Listen to your son.'

———

All three were walking by the riverside along a large wooden walkway which was in front of the horseshoe-shaped luxury apartment complex. In the centre was a shared garden that looked onto the Thames. It was a world away from the council estates and bedsits that they had stayed in. Rebwar wondered if Bijan was creating a little harem for himself. If that was who she was seeing.

'Dad, Dad, can I go and see Ariana Grande? She's playing over there.' Musa pointed at the big dome across the water which was the O2 centre. 'And you know it was a James Bond. So dope.'

Hourieh slapped his head. 'Language.'

Rebwar laughed. He had missed these family moments. He'd conveniently ignored them and even tried to forget.

'Nice place. You working?' said Rebwar.

'No, but looking. Had some offers, but they were no good jobs. I want a career.'

'We all have to start somewhere.'

'What do you know about a career? Look at you. Security guard? What has happened to you?'

'And you...' Rebwar gritted his teeth. 'Where did you get those Peroxy boxes?'

Musa went over to the edge of the walkway and looked over the river.

'He's a good kid, I'm proud that you've managed to keep him on track. Must be difficult.'

'Look, I want a divorce.'

Rebwar stopped and offered her a cigarette. 'Can we try to work it out first? Talk. Try again?'

'Why? I have a new life here.'

'And what is that? Living in a harem with... with—'

'Bijan? Yes, he has been good to us. You can't provide and I need to look for other options.'

'Well, at least tell me what happened on that night. And, I'll bloody give you a divorce. Deal?'

Hourieh spat on her hand and held it out. Rebwar felt nervous. This was a point of no return. Honour was involved.

'I still love you.'

Hourieh looked stern, just wanting to move on. She was as stubborn as a mule. She looked down at her waiting hand.

Rebwar shook it firmly.

'Hey, guys, have you sorted it out?' said Musa running back.

Hourieh turned away and wiped her eye.

Rebwar brought out a ten-pound note from his wallet. 'Saw that there are a few shops over there. Fancy getting us two coffees and get yourself something.' He gave him another ten. 'In case there's something nice.'

Musa ran off, skipping every other step.

'So tell me... all of it.'

Hourieh puffed her cigarette and took a deep breath. 'He was desperate and I should have left him. But, like I said, it was too late. He needed to make money. I helped. It was stupid, but I had to feed my son. It was going to be his last deal... or so he said. He'd said that a few times.'

Rebwar looked at her, desperately trying to keep his mouth shut.

'I know that look, but just listen to me. He made me wait in the car. It was raining, late – maybe ten or something. And Myrian and Vivek appeared. We didn't end on good terms. I, again, stuck up for Amin. I am loyal, you know this. Husba...' Hourieh swallowed. 'They wanted to know where he was and I wasn't going to tell them. I knew they were trying to frame Amin for all the problems they were having. Calling us and trying to sue us. Idiots. And that Myrian...'

Rebwar looked.

'OK, she's a bitch. So yes, Vivek hit me and then all went black.' Hourieh pointed at a scar on her temple. 'He did this and he is still going to pay for it.'

'He's in a coma. His ex-wife nearly burned him alive. It was an accident.'

'Serves him right. Good! Piece of...' Hourieh finished her cigarette and dropped it on the wooden decking. 'Then when I woke again. I was in the car and no Amin and I went to look for him.'

'Where?'

'In the streets around. But I couldn't find him.'

'What did you see?'

'Kids going to bars, buses with people, some Arabs... the usual. I passed a few pubs but not a sign of him. Tried to call him many times. I wanted to call you but I was worried and I was worried about Musa so I drove back.'

'Could you have called Vivek or Myrian?'

'No, they could have found him and, I don't know, he had knocked me out. I was scared.'

Rebwar got a text from Geraldine with a series of photos from Ms Boyd's apartment. He looked at them and zoomed in on the one with the jewellery. 'This earring... is it yours?'

Hourieh got her glasses from her Louis Vuitton handbag. 'No, why?'

'We found your jewellery with Amin and your wedding ring.'

'That, that...' Hourieh looked down. 'I'm not proud but he was going to find money for them.'

'We found the other earring with your jewellery.' Rebwar flicked through the other pictures and saw the burka. 'You said Arabs... a woman in a burka?'

'Yes, saw some men shout to the woman. Like Arabs do.' And Hourieh gesticulated with her hands.

'Idiot!' Rebwar remembered the woman dressed in a burka at Ms Boyd's apartment. 'Thank you for talking, but I have to find this woman in the burka. I think it was her.'

Hourieh laughed. 'You going to arrest all the women wearing burkas?'

'Kiss Musa for me and tell him I love him.' Rebwar turned around and walked off, calling Raj.

FIFTY-TWO

Rebwar was walking towards Blackwall railway station, which was a ten-minute walk from where he had left Hourieh. Raj had logged onto Ms Boyd's laptop and found that it was linked to her mobile and was getting text notifications. She hadn't disabled it or tried to remotely wipe the computer. As she hadn't even set a password for her laptop, Raj guessed she wasn't an IT geek. The last message was a confirmation of her using her bank card on the DLR and furthermore, Raj had found an email with a flight confirmation to Milan from City Airport. The station to which Rebwar was heading was in that direction. He called Geraldine.

'I got your photos. It's Llaria Boyd and she's making a run for it. She's on a DLR train to City Airport. I'm going to try to intercept her.'

'Don't do anything rash. I'm on my way.'

Rebwar ran up the flight of steps that led up to the trains. Once on the platform, he looked for the upcoming trains. The next one was heading to Stratford and he had to wait for the following one bound for Woolwich Arsenal. But he had no idea if he had missed her or she was in the next upcoming carriages. He saw a boxy red and blue train approach. He walked along the platform checking for her in the carriages. By the time he got to the end, the door closed and went off with a stuttering electric whine.

He flipped the cigarette pack and waited for the next arrival. On the LED display the minutes counted down agonisingly and he carried on pacing around. She'd completely fooled him with the disguise, and of course, she hadn't said good evening back in Persian. He'd thought she was just being rude and wondered why she had killed Ms Maddox. He heard the metal rails ping and whistle as the train approached. As it came to a stop, he got on it and scanned the carriage for Ms Boyd, remembering that she could be wearing a disguise.

The DLR trains were made up of a series of connected carriages that you could walk through without interruption. They also had a conductor who operated the doors and departure. The train was driverless. Rebwar made his way to the front, scanning the passengers. They were a cross-section of London businessmen and women, tourists, workmen and the odd family taking in the sights. The train ran on an elevated rail that took you from Bank, Canary Wharf with its skyscrapers and beyond into the Thames Estuary. Since the nineties, most of the old warehouses had been either converted into luxury flats or razed down awaiting new ideas.

Rebwar spotted two women wearing burkas at the front of the train. He made his way towards them. They were sitting where the driver – if there had been one – would have been. The only way he was going to get to see them was to go up and confront the pair. He walked up the aisles to the front till he got to the middle connecting door. He turned around and saw the two women staring up at him. He smiled. 'Have you seen the driver?' The two women looked away. They didn't fit Ms Boyd's description. The train arrived at Canning Town stop and Rebwar got off and waited for the following one. He picked up his phone.

'I've found her—'

'Where?'

Rebwar heard some muffled sounds before Geraldine said. 'Westferry and just set off—'

'I'll wait for you.' Rebwar looked at the map and saw it was a few stations back. 'Front or back?'

'Middle. Wearing a black coat, large designer sunglasses, hat and a black veil.'

'I'll get in the front and we can corner her.' Rebwar waited for the right train, keeping in contact with Geraldine. Finally, the train approached the platform. Rebwar felt nervous. He had his cable ties and if she was ready to fight back, there was going to be a scene. He wondered if the train's conductor had been trained for incidents. The carriages came to a halt, and the doors slid open with a rush of passengers exiting. Rebwar waited and got in with a few other people. He looked down the carriages and saw that at the end was Geraldine standing in the aisle. A bit closer to him in the middle was Ms Boyd sitting looking out of the window with a small case next to her.

She had met him and would probably react as soon as she recognised him. That could work to his advantage as Geraldine could apprehend her from behind. From Canning Town station there were another two stops till London City Airport. Rebwar made his way down the train between the passengers till she saw him. She looked about her, trying to figure out who else was around. Geraldine was still in the end carriage out of sight. The train's conductor was checking the passenger's tickets with an electronic scanner. He was a medium height, greying man with a goatee. Ms Boyd opened her large leather handbag and took out an injector pen. She put the bag over her shoulder and calmly approached the ticket inspector from behind. She grabbed him and held the pen to his neck.

'This is a dangerous sedative and can kill you. Understand?'

People looked around realising something was going on, and it was followed by a crescendo of screams. The conductor held his hands up.

Geraldine put her hands out. 'Please, everybody calm down. I'm a police officer, listen to me. Please calm yourselves and sit down. Please calm down.'

People retreated to the ends of the train. Boyd made the ticket inspector walk to the front end. Rebwar moved out of the way as did everyone else.

'Llaria, listen to me,' said Rebwar. 'I can call you Llaria?'

She carried on leading her hostage forward. 'I need you to take over the train.'

'I'm not authorised to do that. I have to call in.'

'Look, mister...?'

'Ben... Ben Malton.'

'Open that panel and drive this train.'

'Please, I can't, I...'

Still holding the pen on his neck, Llaria got a syringe out of her bag and took off the orange top with her teeth. She pushed him forward and lifted his shirt.

'Don't make a move or you'll never walk again.'

She felt up his spine and injected him. Malton's legs

gave way and she pushed him into the seat facing the control panel.

'What have you done to me?' His face was white with fear. 'I can't... I can't feel my legs, I can't fucking feel my legs!'

Llaria stroked his forehead. 'Nothing to worry about. Women get this all the time. Childbirth, epidural. Now—'

'Llaria, stop before it's too late,' said Rebwar. 'Think about this... carefully.'

'Now, Ben, listen to me. You're going to manually override this train.' Llaria calmly prepped another syringe from a vial she got from her handbag.

Shaking, Ben opened a lid at the front of the train to reveal a series of buttons and levers. He slid a key and turned it.

'Grazie. Take me to the airport and don't stop at the next station.'

Malton's walkie-talkie crackled to life and his name was called.

'Off! Switch it off.' Llaria pressed the pen to his neck and he turned it off.

Geraldine approached Rebwar. 'Any bright ideas?'

'No, but we need to restrain her.'

'Hey, you two, come here. I know you... you a policeman? Attesa helped you.'

'Why did you kill her?'

'She was in the wrong place at the wrong time. Unfortunate.'

'Llaria—'

She stood up. 'Give me your phones.' She held the pen on Malton's thick neck and held out her other hand. 'I'm counting.'

Rebwar and Geraldine gave over their phones. Behind

them, people were holding up their phones, videoing them or on a call. The train passed the Pontoon Dock station. A couple of passengers shouted over to stop.

'Llaria, think about it. We can work it out,' said Geraldine.

'What's your name?'

'Geraldine.'

'NO! Official name.'

'DC Geraldine Smith.'

'When we get to the next station, you're going to make a path for me.'

Rebwar looked around for an opportunity. Malton's eyes fixed on Rebwar like he was trying to tell him something, flickering over to his left. Rebwar saw the handle. Malton looked down twice. The train approached the station.

'Ben, get ready to stop this train,' said Llaria.

He moved his torso to reach for the round button.

Rebwar reached out and pulled the emergency lever. An alarm sounded and lights flickered across the control panel.

Llaria glared at Malton. 'What's going on?'

'Have an emergency. The control room has been contacted—'

'NO! Stop here, now!'

'We're not aligned – we have to be aligned. Otherwise the train won't stop.' Malton pressed some buttons which made the flashing warning signs stop as well as the alarm.

Llaria grabbed his hand. 'Stop! Stop now!'

Malton panicked and flicked some levers which made the train speed up and pass the platform. Llaria screamed and grabbed his shoulder to pull him back. With his left hand, he grabbed the wrist holding the syringe and pulled the key out of the control panel with his right. Llaria used her free hand to take the syringe and plunge it into Malton's thick neck. In the struggle, he threw the keys behind him and his eyes rolled back.

FIFTY-THREE

Rebwar saw the set of keys that Malton had thrown and went back to get them. A large black man picked them up. He had a big black beanie that hid his dreadlocks, his eyes were bloodshot, and his black skin had a sheen on it. His denim jacket barely covered his broad chest.

'Is he dead?'

'No.' Rebwar stepped up to the man. 'I need you to sit down and pass me the keys.'

The man looked over to see Llaria hitting the control panel, trying to drive the train and pointing an injector pen at Geraldine.

The man nudged his way past Rebwar. He grabbed his shoulder. The man turned and flicked Rebwar's hand back and held it there. A bit more pressure and he would break his wrist. 'I've got this.'

'Don't be a hero.'

The man let go of Rebwar's shoulder and stepped forward with the keys. 'Hey, bitch. This ends with me.'

Llaria reached into her handbag and brought out a syringe.

The man laughed. 'What? You're going to prick me to death?'

'Give me the keys and yes I am.'

'Sir, step back,' said Geraldine.

'Love, I've got this. It's time for the men to handle this.'

Geraldine stepped between him and Llaria. 'Sir, step back and let the police handle the situation.'

The train was approaching King George V station. A high-vis wall of police and TfL staff filled the platform. Rebwar looked around for something to disable the man, and all of a sudden it all kicked off.

'Bitch!' said the big man looking down at the syringe lodged in his chest. Geraldine lay on the floor between two seats having been pushed out of the way. The big man stumbled around, lashing out. Llaria got another pen and stuck it into his thick leg. He tried to swear but only managed to mumble. The train began to slow down at the station. Llaria grabbed the keys from the man and inserted them into the control panel. The man was now trying to hold himself up on the metal poles and seats. Rebwar couldn't get past him.

Boyd injected a pen into Malton's neck and slapped his face. 'Hey, are you here, hello?' She slapped his face again.

The train carried on slowing down and the police officers ran up to the windows.

'Hey, Ben, I need you.'

He came to and looked around.

'Drive the train.' Boyd held another pen on his neck. 'Otherwise this time you won't wake up.'

Malton breathed in and reached out for the control panel. Behind them, passengers banged on the windows.

'Come on, pronto, veloce, fast, fast,' said Llaria.

A window exploded, the glass spilling into the carriage.

One of the officers had used his baton to smash it. The train picked up speed. The police officer tried to get into the accelerating train but lost his footing and fell onto the platform. Passengers screamed and shouted.

Geraldine stood up, feeling her bruises and pains.

'Shut up down there, otherwise, I am going to kill this man!' shouted Llaria at the passengers, who sat back down as the train carried on down the track.

'Why did you kill Amin?' said Rebwar.

'How did you find me?'

'Your computer.'

Llaria smiled. 'You stole it? What kind of policeman are you?'

The train headed for a tunnel.

'There's no way out,' said Geraldine. 'This is a dead end.'

The train made its way into the lit tunnel. To the right, running level with the train was a concrete path. Rebwar looked back and saw the passengers pulling the emergency levers.

'One more step and I'll kill him.' Llaria pressed the pen into Malton's sweaty neck.

'What about we release some of the passengers?' said Rebwar. 'We can work something out.'

Llaria stayed silent.

'Think about it. We can negotiate something. There's mothers and children. They'll be willing to help.'

Boyd nodded and said. 'Stop the train.'

Malton operated the control panel and the train came to a halt.

'What about him?' Rebwar pointed at the man with dreadlocks slumped over the seat.

'Ben, call your boss.'

Malton reached for his walkie talkie and switched it on. 'Malton to Control, over.'

'Malton, fuckin... sorry. Control here, what's the status?'

'Mate, I've had better days. I've got a situation. The train's stopped and we have a hostage situation, over.'

'Oh... Ben, stay calm... we'll get some help... over and out.'

'Excuse me! Hey, excuse me,' said a passenger at the other end of the train. 'What's going on?'

'We're going back to the airport,' said Llaria.

A man with a hoodie bolted over to the broken window and jumped out onto the emergency walkway and ran off back up towards the station. Others followed. Llaria fidgeted and wanted to shout something but the passengers were taking the initiative to run. The doors opened. Llaria looked down at Malton. He had done it. She screamed and hit him with the pen and punched him with her fists. It wasn't long before he was unconscious.

Geraldine and Rebwar stepped back; Llaria's raw anger was all too visible. Rebwar looked back and saw that the train was now empty – the passengers had all fled.

The walkie-talkie crackled. 'Control to Malton, over.' They all looked at it lying on the floor waiting for someone to pick it up. Llaria got there first and stuck out her pen at them. She switched it off.

'Tell me about Aahil,' said Rebwar.

Llaria's face froze for a moment and her eyes stared at Rebwar.

'What happened?' said Geraldine. 'Is that why you killed Amin?'

'He was a bastard, but you know that.' She stood up and looked through her handbag to bring out a picture of Aahil and showed it to them. It was of them on a beach promenade, both smiling, with a blue sky and sand. 'He killed him, not me. He was a butcher and lying son of a bitch.' She looked at the picture of Aahil and rubbed her eyes.

'What happened with Amin?'

'He was a coward and an excuse for a man. Bastardo. Used women as objects.'

'And Aahil?'

'He was weak... I tried.'

'I've been there,' said Geraldine. 'You try to help them. But they can't help themselves.'

'What do you know?'

'My ex. She was a user.'

'But Aahil was a victim of Amin like me. He needed to be stopped. And I did it.'

'And Steve Buckham?' Rebwar took out a pack of cigarettes.

'Who?'

'He sold drugs to Amin.'

Rebwar offered Llaria a cigarette.

'Did you push them down the manhole?' said Geraldine.

She nodded.

The lights went out and a few seconds later a couple of emergency lights came on. It was still dark.

Llaria stood up and looked around.

'Are they OK?' Geraldine pointed at Malton and the big man.

She just shrugged. Geraldine went over to the black man to check for a pulse.

'Get off him.'

Geraldine carried on and picked up his arm. Llaria stabbed her in her neck with the pen. Rebwar punched

Llaria on her nose. Her head jolted back and she slumped down into the corner by the control panel and Malton.

'Are you OK?'

Geraldine held her neck and struggled to stand up. Rebwar tried to help her but couldn't hold her between the seats and metal poles. She fell onto the floor. Rebwar could hear some movement coming from the corner. A couple of glass vials rolled under the seat. Rebwar picked one up and read its label. Alcuronium Chloride for injection. He got up and saw Llaria with another loaded syringe.

'Llaria, listen to me.'

Her nose was broken and bleeding and she wiped some of the blood away from her mouth.

'You did what you needed to do. Now stop, understand? And you can still save yourself and them. They are innocent.'

Llaria shook her head and spat out some blood. 'No. We are all born with sin. I can see that you have sinned. But I sinned for the good.'

Rebwar heard footsteps echoing in the tunnel. Somebody switched the electricity off to storm the train. He had to buy some more time. He leant down to feel Geraldine's neck. There was still a faint pulse.

'Llaria, there's nowhere else to run. You can do some good now. Just save Ben, Geraldine and this man.'

She looked at them and stuck the needle straight into her own chest then pressed the plunger. Her breathing became erratic and she collapsed onto the floor. Rebwar ran out onto the pathway and shouted for the emergency personnel to come over.

FIFTY-FOUR

Geraldine was at the London Mithraeum in the Bloomberg building, it was between the Bank and Cannon Street tube stations. She had never heard of the museum, which featured the remains of a Roman temple. This wasn't your typical light airy place but a dark cavern. She walked around looking at a tall white cabinet of artefacts. Ancient history wasn't her thing. To her, it looked like a collection of odd broken pottery and rusting scrap metal. She carried on looking for Highclere. The main attraction was the temple itself and it looked more like the remnants of a foundation than a grand hall for religious ceremonies. She was surprised by how small it was. You could walk around its exterior on a raised walkway. A series of lights projected onto a fine mesh, which reflected a ghostly image of how the temple walls had once looked.

Highclere stood behind what was left of the altar in his usual three-piece suit; this one was navy blue, and he wore a black shirt with tan leather brogues and the inevitable sunglasses. Geraldine walked up to him.

'What's this place?'

'A temple to Mithras.'

Geraldine waited for him to go on but he leaned on the glass bannister facing the temple. 'And he was?'

'We don't really know. Mithraicism was an underground cult with a god who slaughtered bulls. They built their church under other buildings. To the people they represented caves. And it was an area for initiation for souls to descend and exit.'

Geraldine shivered.

'Not into the theology and old beliefs? Mithraeum, they're a bit like us. An underground organisation.'

'So, what's the order of—'

'This...' Highclere brought a brown envelope out of his pocket. 'There's the payment and a job.'

She opened the flap and looked in. There was a wad of cash in a zip-locked bag with some powder and a couple of USB drives. 'What am I supposed to do with this?'

'We still have a problem with DS Hunter. He's like a dog with a bone. You should have let him catch the killer. Alive.'

'She was about to catch a plane and get away.'

Highclere walked off around the ruin. 'Frankly, that would have been preferable.'

Geraldine followed him. The place was empty but felt stuffy, which made her uncomfortable. 'I don't get it... He would have wanted to arrest someone for the murder.'

'You could have found a fall guy... those doctors.' At the opposite end of the building was a glass walkway that extended over the entrance of the temple. Highclere walked to the end, and she followed. The suspended platform gave a view and feel of being inside the temple. Geraldine felt a little uneasy.

'What's the job?'

'There is compromising data, counterfeit money, drugs...' Highclere looked at the scene and breathed in. 'I'll let you take the initiative. Just fix the problem you've made.'

For a moment Geraldine felt like pushing him over into the chasm, the cracked leftovers of what was once a stone floor. She just wanted him to grow a pair and confront DS Hunter. He smiled. Geraldine turned around and left.

———

It was as if she had found another crypt beside the museum. But Gordon's wine bar was just off the embankment by the Thames and in the basement of one of the imposing buildings that overlooked Victoria Embankment gardens. Geraldine sat with a bottle of red wine and two glasses. It had an original Dickensian-style decor and the well-worn panels were covered with framed pictures of old newspaper articles and Victorian-era paintings. The whole place felt like it was being held together by the flaking varnish and layers of black paint. Pipes and electric cables had been attached to the walls and ceilings like a spider would have woven its home. She poured herself a large glass of wine and gulped it down. It had all caught up with her and she felt empty. She stretched out her legs over the stone floor.

'What is this place?'

She looked behind her to see Rebwar and motioned for him to sit down.

'I see you've had a head start.'

Geraldine poured him a glass of red wine.

'Red? This must be serious.' He grabbed the bottle and looked at the label.

'Fancied a change. It's a good place to get drunk.' She raised her glass.

Rebwar clinked her glass. 'Cheers! What's the occasion?'

'Highclere, fucking us about.' And she pushed over the brown envelope.

Rebwar picked it up, looked into it and frowned, 'For us?'

Geraldine shook her head. 'For cleaning his fuck up, or that's what I think – or at least someone's.' She finished her glass of wine. 'I'm tired. How's the wife?'

'She wants a divorce.'

'Fuck. Sorry to hear. Why? Sorry. Stupid question...'

'What am I supposed to do with this?'

'DS Hunter... we need to set him up and you can have some of the money – it's fake. I'm tempted to turn it all on Highclere.'

'How's Beckie?'

Geraldine shrugged her shoulders.

'Still in hospital?'

She looked down at her shoes and blew a raspberry.

'Nice wine. Did you hear the one about the Iranian king and his daughter, the princess?'

Geraldine looked up. 'No.'

'The king had been born blind and when his daughter reached puberty, everyone gossiped about how beautiful she was and they would pay with their lives to sleep with her.'

She refilled the glasses.

'So in his rage, he decided to set a challenge for his subjects and asked for a wooden box to be built that could fit his largest lion and a man. And whoever could wrestle the lion and kill it with his bare hands, they could sleep with his daughter.'

'And I thought it was going to be a dad joke.'

'For days, men lined up to take the challenge and they

all failed. On the fifth day, a Turkish man arrived. He stepped into the box and deep growls and grunts rocked the wooden crate. And after a long tense hour, the man stepped out of the crate, went up to the king and asked, who do I have to kill?'

Geraldine smiled. 'I going to need some shots.'

Rebwar's phone buzzed and he brought it out of his pocket. On reading his text he smiled. 'My son has got tickets for a Chelsea match.'

'Finally, some good news.' And she got up and headed for the bar.

FIFTY-FIVE

Rebwar sat with Musa at The Shed End at Stamford Bridge Stadium. Around them was a sea of blue and white, Chelsea fans wearing their team colours. Rebwar had bought Musa a scarf which he wore proudly. The atmosphere was electric and full of anticipation. They were playing one of their old local rivals, Tottenham Hotspur. So far they were on an eighteen match unbeaten run since the beginning of the season and in a combative mood, as they had also beaten their other London rivals, Arsenal. Musa unzipped his jacket to reveal his T-shirt. Rebwar smiled and read the text. It had a headline saying Match tactics and below, three boxes each linked with an arrow, the first one said kick off, the second one pass to Morata and the third asked did he score? Next to it were two options of yes or no. With no pointing to the box pass to Morata and yes to kick off.

Rebwar grabbed his son and kissed the top of his head. The crowd erupted into a cheer as the team ran onto the pitch. People shouted players' names and taunts to the opposing team. It was all going to kick off.

'So tell me again how you got the tickets?'

Musa looked up to him. 'Came in the mail. Sure Bijan sent them.' He passed him the envelope again.

Rebwar saw that it was addressed to the New Providence Wharf apartment where Hourieh and Katarena were living. Which only he and Bijan knew. There had been no note, and the address had been typed out. The postmark was very faint and he could only make out the word, London.

'They are playing four-three-three.'

'And Spurs?'

'Unusual, four, one, two, one, two.' Rebwar's phone rang, it was from a withheld number. He picked it up. 'Hello?'

'Hello, my friend.'

'Who is this?' Rebwar used his left hand to cover his ear and block out the loud cheering.

'An old friend. How's the match going?'

Rebwar looked up to see one of the Spurs player's head in a goal. There was an immediate cheer from the stand opposite and groans from around him.

'It was me who sent you the tickets.'

Rebwar couldn't make out who it was. 'Who?'

'Your old friend Farrouk.'

Rebwar felt a cold chill. The noise of the crowds faded away and he sat down. 'Farrouk?'

'You thought I was dead... I'm on your home turf.'

DID YOU ENJOY THE BOOK?

Thank you for reading my book and hope you enjoyed as much I did writing it. If you could find a moment to leave a review for which I would be eternally grateful for. This helps other readers to find this book and share the buzz. It only has to be a few words, a rating or even a helpful vote on a reviewer's comments. It all helps us indie authors to get the word out.

ALSO BY OLS SCHABER

The Contact

Sign up at www.olsschaber.com and get your free novella.

A prequel to the Rebwar series where we meet his first contact Clive. A dramatic inciting incident sets off a chain of events where Rebwar is left to pick up the pieces.

Rebwar - The Missing Parts

(Book 1)

Ex-Iranian police detective Rebwar hides from his past behind the wheel of his London Uber. But when an enigmatic organisation threatens to expose his identity, he has no choice but to lend them his skills. And when his missing persons assignment leads only to a severed foot, he'll have to connect it to a body to prevent being deported.

When he finds his quarry's wife in bed with another man, Rebwar is forced to revive his old interrogation methods to extract a confession. But when the case is closed despite body parts still appearing, he's convinced there is more to the murder than his superiors want known. Determined to learn the truth, his private investigation uncovers a conspiracy that could see him torn to pieces

The Gipsy

(Book 2)

Rebwar struggles to recover from his last brutal case. But with his illegal migrant status used by his shadow organisation bosses to hold him under their thumb, he's stuck working at an East End car wash... until the owner is gunned down before his eyes. And when his handler wants him to find out why, he's forced back into the underbelly of the city's deadliest streets.

Going undercover as a delivery man, Rebwar follows the clues to a disturbing human-trafficking operation. But when he runs into an old adversary willing to get their hands dirty, the desperate military man worries he's walking right into an unmarked grave.

Can Rebwar destroy a smuggling ring before he's the next to eat a bullet?

Rebwar - Plan B

(Book 3)

Iranian ex-detective Rebwar still struggles to gain his footing in London. Barely making ends meet driving an Uber, he can't keep his marriage from fraying. And when the shadowy agency blackmailing him orders an investigation into one of their own, he's caught between domestic stress and clandestine murder.

In over his head when a key political figure is killed, Rebwar walks a knife's edge of danger pursuing the truth. But when his main informant disappears, he exposes a plot for him to take a fatal fall.

Can Rebwar finally unmask his sinister employers before he loses his family... and his life?

Ols Schaber, The Missing Parts: Rebwar. Kindle Edition.

ACKNOWLEDGMENTS

I must thank the people around me that have made this series possible. I feel so lucky to have them there and they encourage me to keep going. It's quite an undertaking writing a good yarn and even more to self publish. I couldn't have done it without them. My amazing wife Tracey, to my editor Ed Handyside, my brother Fred, and so many other great friends. You know who you are.

NOTES

Chapter 25

1. Whore

Chapter 46

1. Barmieh are small doughnuts that are infused with saffron, rosewater and syrup.
2. Good evening.